THE CRIMSON ARROW

SAM GALLENBERGER

Table of Contents

"Thank you, Detective. We'll take it from here."

Special Agent Walt Zbysko stood in the small barn's doorway and scanned the dimly lit interior. The stench of death was strong. Dusk fell on an ancient wood floor, covered in dust and disturbed by numerous footprints. Shafts of light streamed from cracks in a sagging roof.

Long abandoned. A natural choice.

"With all due respect, Agent Zbysko, my team is here," the detective replied. "They can work the scene."

"But they won't, Detective Tomlinson."

Zbysko turned his head slowly, taking it all in.

A single window with dirty, tinted panes, crowded by empty cobwebs. A dust-covered wooden bucket rested in the corner, its rusted handle covered with filth. An old worktable sat to the left, near the far wall.

All unsurprising. All but what had brought Walt.

The woman's body was glued to the wall to his left, arms wide, wrists limp. Like the others.

"With all due respect..." The detective's voice edged in on Walt's thoughts. Tomlinson was still here.

Walt looked over his left shoulder to where Nikki Holden, whose badge read forensic psychologist, stood staring at the woman's body. She caught his get-rid-of-the-cop glance and turned to face Detective Tomlinson. Walt returned his gaze to the shed's interior as she spoke.

"I'm sorry, Detective," she said in her most reasonable tone of voice, "But I'm sure you can appreciate our position here. Give my team a few hours. If this isn't our guy, you'll be the first to know. The police department's been more than helpful."

Walt looked up to mask his knowing grin.

"I don't like it," Tomlinson said. "For the record."

Walt pulled his eyes from the crime scene and smiled at the detective. "Thank you, Detective. Noted. There's quite a bit about this job not to like. If your men could secure the perimeter, that would be helpful. Our forensics team has arrived."

Tomlinson held his gaze for a moment, then turned away and addressed a man behind him. "Okay, you, cancel the forensics, this is now a special investigation. Tell someone to secure and hold the perimeter."

The man muttered a curse and flicked away a bit of straw he'd taken from a pile of old bales. A white unmarked van rolled over the yellow perimeter tape and slowly crunched the gravel on the driveway.

Walt glanced at Nikki. "Tell them to start on the outside," he said flatly. "Give us a minute. Bring Kim in when she arrives."

Nikki headed for the van without comment.

Walt turned his attention back to the small barn. The killer's nest. The rest of the story was here, in the dark corners.

The walls had watched the killer as he'd methodically ended a woman's life. The worktable had heard his words as he confessed his passions and fears in a world turned inside out by his compulsions. It had witnessed her pleas for mercy. Her dying moans.

Careful not to step on the exposed markings in the dust, Walt entered the room and approached the wall on which the woman was affixed. He stood still, filtering out the sounds of voices from a dozen law enforcement personnel outside. The hum of rubber on asphalt from the main road a hundred yards down the driveway settled in with the sound of his breathing. Both faded entirely as he brought his senses in line with the scene before him.

Her nude torso rose pale in the glow of a single light shaft. An arm stretched out to either side. Two round dowels that supported much of her weight protruded from the wall through her wrists. Taking a step back, he realized her appearance seemed to form a "Y."

A white veil of translucent lace had been carefully arranged to cover her face, like a bride.

The outthrust posture sent a collage of art-history remnants cascading through his mind — the *Venus de Milo,* a thousand renditions of the Crucifixion, the Louvre's *Winged Victory* statue, her marble bosom jutting forward as if it belonged on the prow of an ancient ship plowing through a Mediterranean surf.

However, this was no museum. It was a crime scene, and the mixture of cruelty and ostentation pouring from the garish exhibit filled him with a sudden wave of nausea.

Slowly, his analytical faculties began to reassert themselves.

She was naked except for thin cotton underwear and the veil. Brunette. White. Early twenties.

Her head slumped gently to the left so that her hair cascaded over her left shoulder before curling under her armpit. Through the veil he could see that her eyes were closed. No blemish, no sign of pain or suffering, no blood. Except for the dagger protruding from her heart.

Only blessed peace and beauty. She could as easily be an angel painted by the world's finest. The perfect bride.

Seth Roland, twenty-four, had brought his girlfriend here after work for reasons unrevealed and found the Slayer's third victim.

Walt peered closer and felt strange words of empathy well up inside of him.

I cry with you, Angel. I weep for you. For every strand of hair that will never again blow in the wind, for every smile that will never brighten someone else's day, for every look of desire that will never quicken another man's pulse. I am so sorry.

"She's beautiful," Nikki said behind him.

He felt a momentary stab of regret for having been pulled away from his connection with the woman on the wall. Nikki walked past him, eyes fixed on the woman, touching his arm gently with her fingers as she passed. Her breathing was steady, slightly thicker than usual. He knew the cause: the dark waters of the killer's mind, which she now probed by staring at his handiwork.

"What a shame." Kim's voice cut softly through the room, grasping what the other two were too proud to verbalize. She stepped up next to Walt, withdrew a pair of white gloves from her bag, then set it down. "What do we know?"

Walt would have preferred to spend more time alone with the victim, but the opportunity had passed. "No ID. Discovered an hour ago by two lovebirds."

They stared in a moment of silence.

"She's beautiful," Kim said.

"Yes."

"This makes three."

"Looks like it, doesn't it?"

She approached Nikki, who remained quiet, lost in thought as she studied the body with searching eyes.

Kim sank to one heel and gently lifted the woman's toes for a better view under the foot. "Care to tell us how you think it happened before I begin my preliminary examination?"

He wasn't ready, of course, not yet, not without a complete analysis of evidence still to be gathered. That said, overcoming that was the job at hand.

"Male, size eleven by the shoe prints. Knowing our assailant, they were likely planted and will be of no use to us. The killer and victim were here for awhile, maybe a day…"

"How so?" Nikki asked.

A distant murmur carried to him: an officer speaking to the curious driver of an approaching car outside, instructing him to head back to the main road. The roof over their heads ticked as it began to cool in the late afternoon.

"He stabbed her in the heart. Yet the place is spotless. He cleaned the body up and spent time meticulously displaying it like this. That takes time."

"Was she alive when he brought her here?"

"Yes. No struggle. A tarp under the table caught most of the trace evidence—bodily fluids, skin cells, hair. He was careful not to use too much force, keeping her on the edge of control and submission. She was lying prone, sedated, conscious and unlikely aware when he first drugged her. He was forced to clean up the blood on the table and floor where it ran off the tarp. Then he sealed the wound, lifted her into position, and placed her on the wall for all to see.

The physical evidence had painted a picture in his mind as clearly as if he were staring at a Rembrandt.

"He did it out of respect, not rage," Walt said.

"Love," Nikki said.

He nodded, even willing to go that far. "Love."

"Same drug as the others," Kim said, standing. "And what kind of love is this?"

"The groom's love," Walt said, savoring his response.

An officer spoke from the door. "Sir?"

Walt held up his hand without looking back. "Give us a few more minutes, George."

The officer retreated.

Kim continued her initial examination, gently prodding the woman's flesh, checking her eyes, lifting her hair, inspecting the backs of her shoulders.

Walt couldn't help but wonder. Why? What motivated the Slayer? How did he make his selections? What good or evil did he think he was doing?

What, if anything, had been done to him to motivate his taking of life in such a manner? Who had he decided to kill next? When would he take her?

Where was he now?

The questions spun through Walt's mind as one, yet distinguishable. Some were clearer than others, but all whispered from beyond, tempting him to listen because each question already contained an answer. He simply had to find it and unpack it.

Nikki paced with one arm pressed against her belly, the other propping up her chin. It struck him that like her, the other victims had been brunettes.

What would enter the killer's mind if he were staring at Nikki through a hole in the wall at this moment? Walt pushed back a fleeting impulse to check the wall behind them to see if there might indeed be a hole, filled with a single eye peering in at them.

Would the killer feel any desire?

No. No, it wasn't desire, was it? She was beautiful, but beautiful women filled the world. Something else drew the Slayer, in the same way that something else was drawing Walt now, though he had a difficult time putting a finger on it.

This would excite the killer, wouldn't it? And if Nikki came on to the killer, would that excite him?

"He would like you," Walt said instinctively.

Nikki glanced back at him, arm still around her waist. "Excuse me?"

He caught himself. This was one of those frequent times when honesty might not be so wise.

"I was just thinking that he liked her. You. That is, speaking to the victim. He. He would like you, meaning he would like her."

Kim saved him. "Speaking to cadavers now, Walt? Don't worry, I do it all the time."

"You were looking at me when you said it," Nikki said.

"So I was. I tend to do that."

"What, stare at women? Or specifically at me?"

"Both, on occasion."

A faint smile turned the corners of her mouth up.

Nikki turned to face the wall, leaving Walt red-faced.

Silence. Remorse. Shame.

"Sir?" an officer's voice intruded again.

Walt turned from the wall and walked to the door. "Bring the team in. Photograph every inch, dust every exposed surface. Blood, sweat, spittle, hair; bag and tag the air if you have to. I want preliminaries from the lab this evening."

"Um…it's getting late. I don't—"

"He's staring through a peephole at another woman already, officer. Furthermore, I need to know what he's stolen. The last two victims had something taken from them. Preliminaries tonight."

TERRORS OF THE NIGHT

These nights were common in the city of Mazono. Doors bolted shut against the terrors of the night, and even the most daring citizen was home with locks in place and alarms activated.

This had just dawned on Shelly Davidson. A quick glance at the clock told her that it was 8:26 pm. Crap, it's late. Too late. Stealing glances around, she noticed that all the surrounding shops had been locked, their salesmen probably tucked behind locked doors in their homes. She frowned and hefted her backpack across her shoulder.

If only Mrs. Liu hadn't dawdled over the items she wanted to purchase. That cantankerous old woman always had a complaint to make about something. "I remember when Mazono was beautiful," or "You didn't need to lock your doors back then," she'd say. Attending to Mrs. Liu was always a chore. Shelly had been only too happy when the woman had finally shuffled out of the shop, and she had been able to complete her closing routine.

That led to her current predicament. The sun had set, and a light breeze picked up. She increased her pace, sending furtive looks around her.

She took a deep breath as she approached Charlie's, the bar that was only a few blocks from her house. The place was bustling with activity. A number of men were leaning against the wall, some staring into space, some looking directly at her. As Shelly jogged past, she noticed another man lay unconscious on the pavement while a few others shuffled through the cash they had relieved him of.

"Hey, sweetheart!" one of the other men called out to Shelly. "Care to warm my bed tonight? I'll be good to you if you're good to me!" The laughter of the other men rang in her ears as she continued to jog past.

She had to get home. The walk to her house, usually only about fifteen minutes, now seemed to be taking an interminably long time. She was at the alley just before her street when hands came out of the shadows and grabbed her. The feel of something sharp pressing against her neck stifled her scream. She whimpered as her assailant added pressure on the knife. The feel of warm blood flowing down her neck quieted all her thoughts of struggling.

"Hello, beautiful," a raspy voice said. The fumes of the man's breath blew over her face. "I just need some cash, y'know?" Without a word, she handed over her purse to her assailant. "Good girl," he whispered. She heard a thud as her bag fell to the ground. Shelly's face turned pale. The man then leaned forward to smell her neck. "You smell so good…so good…and it is a cold night…" Shelly bit her lips as the man's hand started to run over her body. Instinctively, her hand reached out to hold his.

"Please," she begged in a trembling voice. "Please, don't."

"Why not?" came the reply. "Don't worry. I'll be good. Real good." His hand sneaked under her sweater and firmly gripped her breast, while the other hand kept the knife to her throat. Shelly closed her eyes. It wasn't enough to hold back the tears flowing down her face.

Her mind wandered to Josh, her boyfriend. If only he were here, he could protect her. Would she ever see him again? Would he even want her after this? Only just this morning he'd been warning her about the dangers of…that's it!

"You promise you'll take care of me, baby?" Moving as carefully as possible, she slowly moved her hand down towards her jean pocket.

"I wouldn't lie to you, beautiful," he said, eyes beaming. Her assailant didn't take notice as he forcefully kissed the side of her neck.

She reached around a little further before grabbing hold of what she was looking for. Okay, wait for it. The knife loosened against her neck, and instantly, she pushed the man back and sprayed a generous portion of liquid in his eyes. The man's scream of pain and rage was all the motivation she needed to pick up her bag and run for all she was worth. She made it into her apartment, where she promptly locked her door behind her. She collapsed behind it, tears flowing down her face and body trembling.

"Well hey there, Barn!" Johnny said as he slapped his friend on the shoulder. The dirty blond in the leather jacket turned around smiling.

"Johnny Boy!"

"Ready to take a beating?" Johnny asked, smirking.

Barney scoffed. "It's always fun taking that ego of yours down a peg," he replied as he adjusted his glasses.

The two men each picked up a pool cue and moved towards a table. Surrounding patrons' eyes drifted towards the two as Johnny took off his jacket. He ran his hands through his light brown hair before taking a seat.

"You'd think they'd be used to us playing here by now," Johnny said.

"Let's be honest, you love the attention," Barney replied.

"Oh shut up."

"Oh, look. Here comes another adoring fan."

Johnny rolled his eyes. As if on cue, a frat boy walked up to them.

"Mr. Carmichael, can I get a selfie?"

"Are you sure you don't want one with my pal Barney? He'll be a big tech star in a few years," Johnny quipped back.

"Uhh no thanks, bro. I'm just trying to look cool for those chicks over there." He motioned his eyes towards a pair of girls watching from across the room.

He sighed. "Sure, kid."

A big grin filled his face, and with his new selfie in hand, the boy bolted off towards the pair of ladies across the room. Barney looked at his watch. "April is running late tonight," he commented.

"Yeah," Johnny replied, examining the cue in front of him. "She called to say she won't be coming. One of her friends got attacked last night, so she's over at our place."

"Oh?" Barney replied. "Who?"

"Shelly."

"Davidson? The brunette who lives in the Backstreets?"

"That's the one."

"What happened?"

"What do you think happened? It's the Backstreets. She was jumped," Johnny replied, and then bent over to shoot a ball. "Some thug came after her with a knife on her way home from work. Luckily your sister has her back."

Barney swore, and Johnny straightened up to face him.

"Easy, buddy. She wasn't hurt. Just shaken up. From what I hear, she gave the dude an eyeful of pepper spray." He sneered. "I wish I had been there to see that dirt bag get blinded."

"It's not funny, Johnny," Barney said. "That's a big deal. Don't you think it's a problem that we are so used to this it doesn't even phase you?"

"Well, what would you have anybody do?" Johnny asked as he passed the cue stick to his friend. "Don a costume and go on a rampage of justice like the Judge?"

"You've wanted to do that ever since we were kids," Barney supplied.

"That's because I'd be an awesome superhero. Seriously Barn, if he couldn't make any lasting impact, who can? As long as we keep our close ones safe, it is what it is. The good ol' days everyone keeps blabbering about are over. Mazono is a shithole now. As long as you don't forget your pepper spray, you'll be fine." Johnny laughed.

"The Judge did a lot to inspire people in this city, Johnny. Laugh all you want, but we could use more people like him these days. The police here are either inept, corrupt, or both." Barney smirked as his last shot went in. "Besides, I'd be screwed if there was a real threat and you were the only one around. You'd freeze up like during that last fight of yours."

Johnny scoffed and collected the proffered stick. "Low blow Barn...low blow."

Barney began to say something but stopped as his eyes made their way to the television. He watched carefully as the newscaster announced the 30th anniversary of the incarceration of Mr. Goode, the man responsible for the Mazono Massacre.

He watched as interviews were conducted with the families of Mr. Goode's victims, as well as those who were lucky enough to escape from him with their lives.

"I don't understand why that man is still alive," Barney said, after the bulletin. "He deserves the chair for all that he did."

"Yeah, well, our justice system is rather squeamish about the death penalty. Life imprisonment is more...humane, you know?" Johnny bent over and made his shot.

"That's exactly my problem with the justice system. It is fatally flawed."

"Take that up with April. She's the lawyer." Johnny sipped some of his beer. "Besides, he's locked away for life. I don't think we need to worry about some psycho grandpa escaping a maximum-security prison. I'm more interested in what happened to the Judge. He kind of just vanished."

"I don't know what happened," Barney replied thoughtfully. "I don't think anybody does."

"Maybe the whole 'keeping the city safe' became too much for him. He was only one man, after all. You've got to have some strong resolve to take that all upon yourself." Johnny groaned as Barney made the winning shot. "Aw, hell."

Barney smiled and patted him on the back. "Drinks are on you tonight!"

"Oh, enjoy your fluke victory while you can," Johnny said good-naturedly. "Don't forget I'm still up in the series."

Barney just laughed.

Later, as they sat with their beer, Barney commented, "I'm serious, Johnny. Something needs to be done about the state of security here."

Johnny rolled his eyes. "You sound like a politician."

"Absolutely not. Sometimes I feel like I wouldn't mind if someone came around and cleaned the streets up the easy way. I don't think any politicians would ever admit to that," Barney said.

Johnny laughed. "Rein in your murderous feelings, man. April and I need you to be at our wedding."

Barney shook his head and started to reply, then stopped. Johnny's playfulness was gone, and in its place was an earnestness that was fierce in its intensity.

"Wedding?"

"Yes, Barney. I intend to ask April to marry me." Johnny looked a little uncertain. He wasn't quite sure what Barney's reaction would be, so he continued.

"I love her, Barney. I love and respect her. I would do anything it takes to make her happy. Do I have your permission?"

Barney shook his head. "You don't need my permission, Johnny. It's ultimately April's decision."

"I know," Johnny felt a weight in his chest at the thought that she might say no, "but I just need to know if you're alright with it. I already asked your dad."

Barney sat back in his chair and looked at his friend. The latter looked back with a combination of hope and anticipation.

"Are you sure about this?"

"Yes, I am," Johnny replied vehemently.

Barney fell silent again. After an unnecessarily long pause, he smiled at his friend. "Of course, you have my permission."

Johnny let out a breath he hadn't even known he was holding. "Thank you, Barney. In light of that, I have one more question to ask of you. Will you be my best man?"

Barney felt his smile grow wider. "Of course!" He raised his tumbler to Johnny. "Here's to a new chapter for both of you."

"If she says yes."

"Oh, she will."

"I hope so." Johnny drummed his fingers on his tumbler, a sure sign that he was disturbed. Barney watched him with fascination. He had never seen his friend quite so anxious about anything before.

"Don't worry," he said reassuringly. "She loves you. I know that for sure." *I doubt you even know just how much*, he added silently.

The next day, Johnny caught a whiff of perfume as he let himself into his apartment after work. Recognizing the fragrance, he smiled. April was home. He followed his nose to the living room where he found her sprawled on the couch, holding a glass of wine and poring over some case files. Her index finger tapped a rhythm on her wineglass, which was a sure sign that she was upset about something. If that wasn't enough, the way she mumbled and the fire he could see burning in her dark eyes told him that she was more than upset: she was flat-out angry.

While she was engrossed in her thoughts, he leaned on the doorjamb and drank in the sight of her. Her lush brown hair had been swept into an untidy ponytail, with tendrils of hair escaping from it. Her face was devoid of makeup, and she was wearing one of his t-shirts with a pair of jean shorts. The glasses she wore, as well as the look of concentration on her face, gave her the look of a teenager working on an assignment. As he watched, she put the wineglass down, swept her glasses up into her hair, and rubbed her eyes in frustration.

With that thought in mind, he pushed back from the doorjamb and cleared his throat. April looked up from the couch with a start, then glared at him.

"What are you trying to do, give me a heart attack? How long have you been standing there?"

"Long enough to watch you pour that second glass of wine, and yes, I've missed you too," he said with a grin, sweeping her into his arms, and kissing her deeply.

"Hmm…" she said, as she tried to regain her bearings. Johnny smiled at her. The reaction was always the same each time he kissed her. He especially loved the way her eyes would come unfocused, and the color on her cheeks would change hue.

"I hope I didn't keep you waiting too long?" he said, as he took off his suit jacket and settled beside her on the couch.

"No, not really," she replied. "Work kept me company." She giggled when he nuzzled her neck. "Oh, stop it, you Neanderthal." She laughed at his answering growl and felt the stress of the day slowly begin to melt out of her system. She sighed and leaned into him. He always had a calming influence on her, even without trying.

"So," he said when he felt her relax against him, "what has kept my lady love so uptight after hours?"

She sighed. "It's Shelly. You remember she got mugged two nights ago?"

"What about her?"

"She has refused to move out of those damn Backstreets. I tried to talk her into moving, but she absolutely refuses to." She let out a frustrated breath. "Nothing I say seems to get through to her. She says she grew up there and she can't leave her family behind." She drew in a deep breath as Johnny's hands began massaging her shoulders in slow, soothing circles.

"Mmmmmm...that feels good...why won't she leave, Johnny? What attraction could those streets possibly hold for her?"

"It's her home," Johnny replied gently. "She's attached to it, has roots there. I guess it's just hard for her to uproot herself."

"Oh, nonsense," April replied irritably. "It was my home too, remember? Mine and Barney's. But we left for a safer part of town. And that's the key issue here: safety. The Backstreets are a hellhole crawling with the worst kind of vermin. It should be totally destroyed, in my opinion. Burnt to the ground till nothing is left standing."

"Good people live there too, April," he reminded her.

"Well, they're fools," she said vehemently. "The Backstreets are no place for a decent person to live. They're just putting themselves and their loved ones in danger. It's stupid." Johnny felt her trembling and held her tighter. "Calm down, April."

"What if you hadn't come at that time, Johnny?" she whispered. "What if you hadn't been there in time to stop them?"

"I was there." He thanked God every day that for once in his life, he did that one thing right. The memory of April's bruises and torn clothes still filled him with rage now, even though he had beaten the two men to within an inch of their lives. He shook his head and kissed her cheek. "I will always be there for you, April. Remember that."

April closed her eyes and savored the warmth his whispered words sent rushing through her. "I know."

After a brief silence, she asked, "Did you ever tell Barney?"

"No. I promised you that I wouldn't."

She was silent for a moment, biting her lower lip. "Thank you."

He was perplexed. "What for?"

"For not telling Barney. I know you guys don't keep any secrets from each other. Thanks for doing this for me."

"April," he whispered fiercely. "I'll do anything for you."

"Johnny…" she said, then turned around to kiss him. He responded, and both of them rode the heady waves of passion.

Later that night, as April slept sated and smiling in Johnny's arms, he let himself fully relive the incident that still tortured him many years after…

It was a dark, windy night. He really shouldn't have been in the Backstreets, but he had been out partying at a club in the neighbourhood and planned to spend the night at Barney's place. He had been in the early stages of intoxication that night; it had been all he could do to stumble through the streets. On getting to the alley just before home, he heard the sound of a scuffle. He prepared to mind his business and go his way when he heard a familiar voice. He stopped and listened. There it was: a female voice, distressed.

Suddenly he felt the adrenaline chase away the cobwebs in his head. It sounded vaguely familiar, the voice. That voice sounded a lot like April's. Sober now, he crept to the edge of the alley and saw one man holding a struggling figure down while the other unbuckled his trousers. The sight drove him temporarily insane, and for the briefest of moments, a red mist blocked his sight, and he felt his blood boil. He remembered charging towards them, but nothing else.

The next few minutes were a blur, but when he came to, April was screaming at him to stop. One man lay on the concrete, bloody and unconscious, and the other lay at Johnny's feet in a battered heap. Breathing hard, he stepped back from the scene, unable to believe what had just happened. Still, the bruises and his blood-soaked knuckles bore testimony to what he had just done. He stifled the urge to give the body at his feet a last, savage kick, and turned to face April.

"Are you okay?"

She nodded, clutching the remnants of her ripped blouse around her. He immediately removed his jacket and wrapped it around her.

"Thank you," she said, trying to still her shivering. "Thank you very much."

He nodded, watching her with concern. He wanted to ask what she was doing outside at this time, but he restrained himself. As if she read his thoughts, she said, "I ended my date early. He should have walked me home."

"He left you to walk back alone through these streets? What an asshole."

"Yeah," she said, before falling silent again.

A few minutes later, she licked her lips and said, a little uncertainly, "Please, could you... could you not tell my brother about this?"

He looked at her, surprised. But he didn't question her.

"Yeah, okay. I won't tell him." He figured she would do so herself when she was ready.

"Thank you," she muttered.

"Don't mention it."

Johnny was drawn back to the present by the feeling of April turning in his arms. He waited until she settled down again, then closed his eyes and let his mind drift back to the past.

MAZONO GARDENS

The room was dark, save for the reading lamp flickering faintly on a worktable. A man moved about absentmindedly, humming a tune. For a moment, he stopped dead in his tracks, then let out a sigh, and continued pacing the room, his bedraggled clothes billowing in the cool night breeze that blew through the open windows.

He moved to the table and sat down. Displayed on the table were newspaper clippings of women in the city. His eyes settled on a particular picture, and he smiled grimly. He raised the picture and levelled his gaze upon it.

It was one of many pictures of the promising young attorney from the newspapers.

She had a certain fierceness to her. With astute diplomacy, she held no prisoners in criticizing the incumbent government of Jack Kennedy, Jr., Mayor of Mazono.

He raised the clipping to his nostrils and inhaled deeply. He imagined the smell of her perfume; intoxicated by it. In the picture, she was at a gala attended by the highfliers of society. The black and white picture did nothing to detract from the simple elegance of her strapless, ankle-length gown, or her impeccably arranged hair. He ogled the faintest hint of cleavage visible through the v-neckline of her gown.

She needed him: that much was obvious. She needed his healing. She needed to be free. Slowly, almost reverently, he added the clipping to the collage of her pictures that were already on his wall and held it in place with a piece of tape.

Then he picked up the syringe sitting on the table and shot a dose of heroin into his system. As the effects of the drug began to take over his system, jarring his senses, he fixed his eyes on her picture.

Only a little while more, my darling, he thought. *Soon you will be free.*

"He's definitely going to propose!" Shelly squealed, laughing.

"Keep your voice down, woman!" April hissed.

"Oh, you know Shelly," Fiona drawled, firing up a cigarette. "Always the drama queen."

It was a Friday night, and April and her friends had decided to have a girls' night in at her place. A box of pizza and four glasses of wine stood on the floor in between them.

"Oh, please!" Shelly exclaimed. "Johnny's going to propose, I just know it!"

April couldn't help laughing at Shelly's excitement. "You're such an incurable romantic, young lady. What if he's just planning something romantic for our anniversary?"

"Or planning to ask you how you feel about a threesome." Fiona scoffed, blowing perfect smoke rings into the air.

"Will somebody tell this chimney to stop poisoning the air for the rest of us?" Clair said, impatiently waving her hand in front of her nose.

"Well, up yours, Clair," Fiona drawled.

"Ladies, ladies," April said before Clair could react, "Let's get back to me, okay? Johnny? Big surprise tomorrow? Super romantic date? Come on girls. Focus."

"Yeah, sorry about that, April," Clair said, glaring at Fiona. "I think I agree with Shelly on this one. Meeting by the angel statue at the gardens is Romance 101. This whole plan sounds like he's working up to a proposal."

April laughed. "I don't know…"

"Oh, April, stop kidding yourself. Have you seen the way the man looks at you? He is completely smitten. You guys are definitely getting married. Yessss!!!" Shelly's voice was raised in excitement.

"This girl must be high on something. Something cheap," Fiona remarked dryly.

"Yes, I'm high on happiness! Got a problem with that?" Shelly asked cheekily.

"Weren't you mugged like two days ago?" Fiona shot back.

"Girls, girls," April cut in. "He invited you all too, you know. Said he'd like our closest friends to be there."

"Ohhhhh…." Shelly said dreamily.

Clair smiled. "It's definitely a proposal, April. Are you ready for this?"

There was silence as she considered the question. Was she ready to be a wife? Was she ready to share the rest of her life with someone, to be bound to one person till death do them part? It was a scary thought.

"I don't know, Clair," she replied. "It's all so...unsettling. So final. Like, you have to spend the rest of your life with this person and just this person. Nobody else. Don't you think it's scary?"

Clair smiled. "It's not so scary if you're sure that you love this person, and you're positively certain that you want to spend the rest of your life with him, in the good times and the bad. Believe me, there will be times when you'll want to kill him for not picking up after himself or leaving the toilet seat up. But trust me, the little annoyances are what make life interesting."

April, looking over at her friend, noticed Clair's eyes were glimmering.

She chewed her lower lip thoughtfully. "I do love him... and I have known him for so long, sometimes it feels like we're already married."

"Then what's the holdup?" Shelly asked.

"You want to be sure," Fiona said as she put out her cigarette and took out a stick of nicotine gum. "And that's admirable, but you guys have been together for most of your adult lives already. What else is there to think about?"

April ran her hand over her face in a thoughtful gesture. "I really don't know," she said. "I'm just scared, I guess."

Clair smiled. "But you love him, right?"

April's reply was immediate: "More than anything."

"Then calm down and let things follow their natural course. Try not to overthink things and just enjoy the moment. You're getting married to the man of your dreams, your best friend. You should savor this moment."

"I should, shouldn't I?" April said, beaming. Suddenly, she shrieked. "I'm getting married!"

"Yes, you are!" Shelly shrieked in reply.

"Let him ask first," Fiona replied, looking longingly at her now empty pack of cigarettes.

"Aww, you're just grumpy because you can't have any more cigarettes," Clair replied cheerfully. The whole group collapsed into giggles, and even Fiona smiled.

He watched from his hidden spot in the bushes, savoring the sight of his beloved raising the wineglass to her lips. A smile enveloped his face. She deserved to be happy. Soon, she would realize that the laughter and joy offered by this earthly realm were without substance: cheap imitations of the real thing.

He scratched at the small hole in his arm. That boyfriend of hers planned to propose. It made everything so much more exciting. He would release her on a symbolic day, saving her from the unfortunate occurrence of being shackled to a mere, unworthy mortal for the rest of her life. Her friends? Mere slaves to do her bidding in the afterlife.

The angel in the garden would be poetic. He would do things differently for her. She was special. Then he would free her, as he had the others.

In so doing, he would divest her of not merely her human form, but of all the weaknesses and flaws that came with it. He would elevate her to a place of spiritual purity. Only then would she be cleansed; only then would she be truly free.

"Ohhh, I cannot believe this is actually happening!" Shelly exclaimed the next day.

They were seated on one of the benches under the city's angel statue in Mazono Gardens, where Johnny had asked them to wait for him. The gardens were surrounded by beautiful gates in every direction. The grounds were well-tended as always.

April remembered coming here for one of her first dates with Johnny. She could picture it vividly. Laughing together for hours, laying on a blanket and watching the stars as it fell dark. Such a happy memory.

The gardens were unusually deserted this evening. Knowing Johnny, he probably rented it out for the occasion. The benches were mostly empty, and in the section where April and her friends sat, the only other person present was a homeless man who was huddled on one of the other benches. His hands held the folds of his ratty, oversized coat around him. His shifty eyes darted now and then in the direction of April and her friends.

"What do you think he's planned?" Shelly asked. She shot a quick glance over to Fiona. Fiona placed her index finger in front of her mouth.

April laughed. "I have no idea," she replied. "I guess we'll all find out together."

"Hey, anybody wondering what's up with this homeless man beside us?" Clair asked in a low voice.

"Yeah, he's creepy," Shelly replied. "How did he even get in here? This is like the safest part of the city. The slums are miles away. Looks like he's been staring at you this whole time too, April."

"Oh, come on, guys. Leave him be. He probably just hasn't had female company in a long time," April replied, as she fidgeted with the hem of her dress. "This is just yet another thing the leadership of this city does wrong: homes should be set up for the rehabilitation of people like this. The streets are dangerous enough without adding the needy and desperate to the mix." Her voice was gradually getting louder.

"Calm down," Fiona replied. "You don't want to look like a shrunken orange peel when your husband-to-be asks you to marry him. Think happy thoughts."

"Yeah, I guess you're right," April replied.

"Still," Shelly replied. "There's something off about this guy. Maybe we should move to another bench." She felt her skin crawl as she remembered a few nights back. "Yes, let's move to a separate bench, please." Her voice was pleading.

"Okay, Shelly," April replied in a gentle voice. The group stood up and moved further away.

He saw one of her friends send another concerned look in his direction and had to bite back a laugh.

Yes, my love, I'm here. Your time to be set free has come.

Then they started heading in the opposite direction. He watched them go and frowned. I've been reckless…I'm giving myself away. *The things you do to me, my dear April.*

He looked around. There were no bystanders within reach. He shrugged to himself. It can't be helped.

He stood up, and with a spring in his step, headed after them.

ALL WAS INDEED PERFECT

Johnny hung up the phone and let out a shaky breath as he approached Mazono Gardens, where he had asked April and her friends to wait for him. The arrangements had been made. Tonight had to be absolutely perfect.

He wanted the day he asked April to marry him to be a memorable one. He sniffed the air and savored the perfume of roses carried on the gentle wind. It seemed even the weather wanted today to be as perfect as possible for him. The evening was calm, and only a gentle breeze was blowing. He smiled. All was indeed perfect.

He turned the corner and paused at the sight in front of him. A man was bending over several bodies, apparently retrieving something from them. Someone was bleeding. Johnny's heart went into overdrive as he saw the glint of a knife.

"*No,*" he breathed. "*April.*"

The man looked in his direction. Johnny caught sight of a mocking sneer before the man took off running.

"No!" Johnny shouted. His vision grew spotty and his stomach churned. He tried to block out the images he was seeing, hoping against hope that the heel he saw and recognized was not April's. *"Dear God,"* he breathed as tears started to mist his vision, *"Please no. Not now. Not like this."* He realized he had lost concentration, and when he once again focused in front of him, the man was no longer visible. He'd simply vanished. *How was that possible?*

Johnny rushed to the bodies and was immediately assailed by the metallic smell of blood. It was so thick that he could almost taste it. His stomach turned over as he saw all of April's friends on the pavement, lying in pools of blood. Over further, directly beneath the angel statue, was April. He bent over and emptied his stomach as tears flowed down his face. When he looked up again, he saw that April lay on her back in a slowly spreading puddle of deep red. Her dress was drenched with it, and so was her hand, which was held loosely to the wound in her chest, to staunch the flow. Her waxy complexion terrified Johnny.

No, no, no.

He ran to April and immediately gathered her close, mindless of the blood. "Stay with me, baby," he whispered, as he brought out his phone and called emergency services. She was still conscious, though her eyes were flickering.

"April," he said, as the tears fell fast. He took off his shirt and used it as a makeshift bandage for the wound. Within seconds his white shirt turned crimson. "Stay with me, baby," he whispered, holding her closer to him. "Please stay with me."

She took a deep breath and opened her mouth to say something. He lowered his head to make out the words.

"I'm...so...rry..."

"No baby, don't say anything. Please. Save your strength."

She shook her head and made a feeble attempt to clutch his arm.

"...not...gonna....make...it."

"Yes, you are," he said, angrily blinking away the tears that were now dimming his vision. "We have the rest of our lives to spend together. Damnit, some creep is not going to take it away!"

She raised her bloody palm to his face, and he felt his blood run cold at the look on hers. It was as if she were taking her final look at him.

"No, April," he said. "Don't say goodbye. This isn't goodbye."

She smiled, her eyes never wavering from his face.

"Yes...my answer...is...yes."

"April," he begged, "Let me ask you properly. Stay with me. Please. I love you. Please stay with me. Please."

Her smile faltered, and tears rolled down her cheeks. He wiped them away with a trembling hand. She gripped it and held his gaze for a long time, her eyes filled with the same light as the day he first told her he loved her. Then her eyes rolled back in her head, and her hand fell limp.

"No!" he shouted as she slumped in his arms. "No!"

The sound of sirens heralded the arrival of the paramedics, who immediately loaded the victims into the ambulance and took them to the nearest hospital. Johnny rode with April, holding her cold hand, praying to every god he could think of. *Please don't let her die. Please. I'll do anything.*

The incessant ringing of his cell phone finally pierced the fog that clouded his mind, and he checked the Caller ID. Barney. He had completely forgotten about him.

Oh God, Barney. How would he take his sister's death?

He immediately shook the thought away. She wouldn't die. She couldn't. She mustn't!

The doctors rushed all four women into surgery the minute they got to the hospital. Barney joined Johnny ten minutes later. The latter was prowling the waiting room, having washed his face and changed his bloody clothing upon request of the nurses. Barney wordlessly walked to him, and the men held each other in a tight embrace. Barney proceeded to sit on one of the chairs, while Johnny continued to stalk the waiting room.

Three hours later, April's doctor came out, a blank expression on his face.

Both men immediately rushed to him.

"Doctor, how is April?" Johnny asked, his heart pounding as he held onto his friend.

"I'm very sorry," he said. "We lost her."

Johnny felt the words like a blow to the stomach. He stumbled to a wall and slid to the ground, fearful that his wobbly legs would no longer be able to support him.

Barney reined in his sorrow enough to ask about the other women.

"I'm really sorry, but two of them were already dead when they got here. One is still alive, but barely. She's in a coma now, and we're not sure if she'll survive."

Barney nodded. "Thank you," he said. He swallowed past the lump in his throat. He couldn't believe it. His mind refused to process what was happening. He had just lost his sister, but he wouldn't give way to his grief. Not quite yet. He walked over to where his friend sat, looking stunned, and sat right beside him, on the floor.

For a long time, they just sat there, saying nothing. Johnny's face was tucked between his knees as endless tears streamed from his eyes, while Barney just sat, staring into space. The grief felt like claws tearing at Barney's insides.

Barney swallowed again, remembering that he had to call his parents. How was he going to do that? Inform them that their baby girl, their only daughter, had just been murdered?

He knew his mother would break if she heard the news. His father was even worse at controlling his emotions. He was almost scared of what his father would do if he knew.

He was startled as he felt movement beside him. Johnny had stood up and was stumbling away like a man in thick darkness. Barney got up and followed him to the parking lot, where Johnny fell to his knees and let out an animalistic howl.

"I'm really sorry for your loss, Johnny," said Carla, holding a handkerchief to her streaming eyes.

"And I yours," he said gently to Fiona's sister. "Thank you for coming," he added. His eyes were unable to meet hers.

"It was the least I could do," Carla replied, her lips trembling. "April was a wonderful woman."

Johnny simply nodded, hugged Carla, and steeled himself for the next sympathizer. It was April's memorial service, two weeks after the incident.

On the other end of the room, Barney stood beside his parents, a somber look on his face. Both parents looked feeble, and tired. Johnny felt his insides tighten as Mrs. Smith raised a handkerchief to already swollen, red-rimmed eyes.

It was his fault the woman was in so much pain. It was his fault that April was dead. If he hadn't come up with the stupid idea of a romantic proposal in the park in this cursed city, she'd still be alive. Even worse, he had frozen, and that moment he lost may have cost April her life.

In a way, he killed her, and that was his cross to bear. Her friends…he remembered the vivaciousness of Shelly, and Fiona's wry humor. He was responsible for their deaths too, and for the death of Shelly's child. She had been a few weeks pregnant at the time of the attack, and her unborn baby had died with her. Clair had come out of her coma only recently and was still in the Intensive Care Unit.

Johnny gritted his teeth. That was his fault too. So much death, and it was all because of him. In a room filled with devastation only Josh, Shelly's boyfriend, was visibly angry. He was in full marine getup. Dealing with loss of those close to you was something he should be used to. However, that hadn't stopped him from breaking down at the other end of the room upon seeing April's body, and storming out. Passing Johnny as he neared the exit, he paused. He turned to look Johnny right in the eyes.

"Fuck you, Johnny. This is all your fault." Then before he could get a response, Josh kept moving and left the church. The faded scar on his cheek was the last thing Johnny saw before he exited the building.

"I know," he said quietly.

The killer watched through the camera he had hidden at a window, watching the people mill about. He watched as Mr. Smith gave a teary-eyed toast, saying that April was the best daughter any parent could ever have. The killer raised his flask, too, fascinated by the oddity of it all.

Fools, he thought. *This should be a celebration! She finally knows the meaning of freedom and they condemn it.*

He watched Johnny, whose face was rendered unreadable by the dark glasses he wore.

I've helped you too, you spoiled, rich brat. You've never known the pain of loss, have you? Well, now you know. Out of these ashes should rise a phoenix: sublime, powerful, invincible. But will you rise above this and become enlightened, you weak fool? I did.

"What do you mean you're calling off the investigation?!" Johnny said, glaring at the man behind the desk.

"Calm down, Johnny. Let's hear what he has to say," Barney said.

The nameplate on the desk read, Detective Jason Walbrick. A ceiling fan swirled weakly above them. The man at the desk maintained a stiff posture. He held April's file in front of him.

"Yes, please keep your voice down, Mr. Carmichael."

"What do you mean keep my voice down?! It's been months since my fia…girlfriend and her friends were murdered in cold blood, and your people haven't even so much as made an arrest. And now you're just going to drop the case?"

"Mr. Carmichael, I would appreciate it if you'd keep your voice down."

"I would appreciate it if you would do your fucking job! Find my girlfriend's killer!"

"I assure you, everything is being done to find him. But like I've already told you, this isn't a regular murder case. The Slayer is resourceful. We've been able to link him to other murders through his preferred method of killing, and so far he hasn't made any slip-up. It's been impossible to catch him. Not only that, but this case doesn't totally fit his MO, as in this case, more than one woman was killed. We aren't calling off the investigation totally, but we need to reallocate our resources a bit. This case will be sent to Special Agent Zbysko."

"So, what have you done on the case? What are you sending to this Zbysko?" Barney asked.

"So far, we've discovered that April was the main target of the attack. Although all the women's hearts were pierced, April was the one laid out under the angel as if she were a prize, meant to be shown off. April also fit the young brunette physical profile of this killer's previous victims, and he'd taken her necklace, as he had taken something from each of his previous victims."

Barney nodded. "Go on."

"For a while, we thought Clair would be the key to a major lead in the case. She survived the attack and saw the assailant up close. However, when she was questioned, she could only give disjointed descriptions of the man that attacked them. All we were able to gather from her was that he was a middle-aged man wearing an oversized old coat, and that he had cruel eyes. That doesn't really narrow things down any." He shook his head, looking disappointed.

Johnny's mind drifted. Clair had left town. She'd begged her husband to take her on the first flight out of Mazono. That had been months ago now. He could still see the fear in her eyes. Since that day, these detectives hadn't been able to come up with anything new.

"Listen, Mr. Carmichael," Detective Walbrick said, "We don't plan to stop looking for the killer. The Slayer is the most wanted man in Mazono. The only thing is that until a new clue is found, we don't have anything to go off of."

Johnny swore ripely and stormed out of the office.

Walbrick placed his elbows on the table and leaned towards Barney.

"Listen, Mr. Smith, I'm really sorry about this, but there's only so much we can do, what with all the budget cuts and limited manpower. Crime doesn't take a holiday, especially in this city. If we spend too much time on one case, many others will go unsolved. That and Zbysko is your best chance at getting this figured out. I hope you understand."

Barney nodded. "Thank you, Detective."

Both men got up and shook hands.

"You're welcome. I'm truly sorry for your loss," he replied.

Outside, Johnny punched the wall of the station again and again. He hated this feeling of powerlessness, of helplessness. The love of his life had been murdered in broad daylight, and there was nothing he could do about it. The rage clawed at his insides, demanding to be let out. No matter what he did, the pain wouldn't go away.

He pulled out his keys and marched towards his car, then looked down at his hands at the blood dripping from his knuckles. He paused for a moment, then put the keys back in his pocket, stalked down the street, and hailed a cab, giving the driver an address. He could at least try to forget.

In the shadiest part of the Backstreets, Johnny got out of the cab and looked up at the sign on the bar. It was one of his old haunts as a teenager. He had gotten into many a barroom brawl while here. He'd stopped at home briefly and chosen clothes he knew would give him an undeniable stench of wealth.

Men lounging in various poses outside the bar snickered at him. *Good*, he thought. *I can't wait.*

He entered the bar and ordered a beer.

Out of the corner of his eye, he saw several men in the room take note of his tailored clothes. He knew that some would remember his face from the TV and newspapers. *Johnny Carmichael, local celebrity.* They would surely think him stupid for coming to this part of town, would dismiss him as a weakling, and try to rough him up. He expected all this; he knew how their minds worked. He ground his teeth. *Bastards. Come and get me.*

He was on his third bottle when one of the regulars approached him.

"What's a man like you doing in a place like this, eh?"

The man's breath was rank with cigarette smoke and alcohol. Johnny continued to drink, ignoring him.

"You think you're too good to answer me, eh, Mister Fancypants?"

Johnny felt a sharp point press into his side. Still, he continued drinking.

The bartender took one look at the madness in Johnny's eyes and called out to the aggressor. "Hey, Ollie…"

"Aw, shut up, Bob," Ollie said. Then leaning over Johnny, he opened his mouth to say something else. The words never made it out.

The first punch drove all the wind out of the man and bent him over. Wheezing, he coughed out expletives and threats. Johnny got to his feet, gave the bartender a hefty tip, and turned back to Ollie. Johnny's second punch echoed throughout the bar as it cracked the man's jaw.

"Anyone else want a piece?" Johnny roared, rolling up his sleeves.

The other men eyed him with hostility. Without a word, another man, who had been sitting next to the first, rushed at him. Johnny neatly sidestepped him and sent him crashing over the counter with his own momentum.

Covered in glass and booze, bellowing with rage, the man came after Johnny again. Again, Johnny used the force of his opponent's momentum to throw him off balance, flipping him up and depositing him onto the table he had come from. The man's body hit the wood hard and when his head whipped back sharply, he stopped moving.

Two other men rushed Johnny at the same time. One held him while the other slammed a fist into his stomach. When Johnny doubled over in pain, the man straightened him up, and punched him in the face, drawing blood.

Johnny aimed a kick at the man's knee, buckling his leg forwards, his victim screaming in pain. Then he threw his head back, smashing the face of the man holding him. Now free, he relished the satisfying sound of breaking bones. Soon the place was in pandemonium, men attacking each other with whatever objects came in handy, and Johnny right in the thick of it.

Finally, the police arrived to break them up, and sent the brawlers home for the night. Johnny shoved a few bills in the palm of the officer in charge and went on his way.

Thunder crashed overhead, and showers began to sprinkle the city as Johnny stumbled along the street, panting. Spitting blood, he pressed ahead, picking up his pace. As the rain strengthened to a torrent, Johnny ran full bore through it, pain and desperation driving him onward.

His clothes grew heavy as he ran, his shoes completely soaked through, but he barely noticed. Thunder rent the air and lightning flashed, but Johnny paid no heed.

Finally, he stopped at the bottom of a hill, climbed over a gate, and then struggled farther forward. His tears mingled with the rain that streamed down his features, as a fierce wind whipped into his face.

A crack of thunder pierced the sky. Johnny trudged past headstones until he found the one he sought, the one he had visited daily for months. Slowly, he sank into a pool of mud on the grave. Feeling nothing but April's loss, he curled into a ball on the ground above her. Then he closed his eyes until, finally, his consciousness faded to black.

The next day, Johnny went to work with a swollen eye and cut lip. The bruise around his eye had turned a purplish black, and could be seen despite the dark sunglasses he wore. He had arrived in sweats, his hair unkempt and nose runny. As he passed his secretary, he snapped out a demand for coffee, then went into his office, slamming the door behind him. Lowering himself into his leather armchair, he dropped his head into his hands. It felt like everything was hurting: his eye, his head, his heart. Last night, he had tried to drown out his misery, but instead, had given himself a cold and destroyed a thousand-dollar outfit. And still his nightmares continued. He seemed doomed to relive April's murder every night in his dreams.

The drinking had not helped one bit. His blood was still boiling, and his heart was still hurting. Would the pain ever go away?

He winced as the door burst open and someone came storming in.

"Go away," he growled. He flinched as the person slammed a newspaper in front of him.

"Barney," he groaned. "Not now."

In the background sounded the soft footfalls of his secretary as she came in the office bearing a tray containing a full coffee pot and two mugs. She nodded to Barney, then placed the tray in front of him and tiptoed out of the office. Johnny reached for the coffee pot and poured himself a cup, still without looking at Barney.

"Your mother called me this morning, Johnny. She's worried about you."

Johnny remained silent, taking gentle sips of the coffee.

"This is the fourth time since the funeral," Barney continued, pointing at what he had slammed on the table. It was a tabloid that had his picture splashed all over the cover. No doubt, it recounted his latest bar fight. He remained silent.

"I know you're hurting," Barney continued. "But this is not the way to deal with it. Getting in bar fights? That is not the answer."

"What is the answer, Barney?" Johnny replied in a low voice. "Her murderer must have come from those slums."

"You really think he's just going to be hanging out at a bar waiting to fight you?"

"Somebody has to pay."

"I agree," Barney replied. "But there's a better way."

"What way? This city has descended to depths of shit I didn't think were possible. April and her friends were killed in plain sight, Barney. Plain sight, and less than a year later the cops have given up. This never would have happened back in the day. The Judge would have stopped it. Instead, the monster who did this is still out there, living a free life, while every day I wake up and see her everywhere I go. I fight because it's the only time I get to feel something, something that isn't anguish over the loss of my fucking fiancée."

"Do you think I'm not hurting just as much as you are?" Barney replied, tears streaming from his eyes. "I lost my sister. My only sister. Do you think I don't feel pain every time I dial her number, then remember that she can no longer answer the phone? Do you think I don't grieve every night? She might have been your girlfriend, Johnny, but she was my sister."

Johnny fell silent. He noticed that his friend was looking rather gaunt, and pale. He saw the bleak look in his eyes. He had thought Barney wasn't as hurt as he was following April's death…it turned out that Barney was only better at masking his pain. Dropping his head, Johnny looked away. Barney continued quietly.

"My dad hit the bottle again. Haven't seen him sober since the funeral. Mom barely talks anymore. We can't sit in a room for more than five minutes before someone starts swearing or crying. We've all been hit hard by this."

After a long pause, Barney continued. "There is an answer. Instead of letting the loss of April stop our lives, we need to honor her.

Johnny looked at his friend.

"This city can't continue like this. I can't continue like this. I'm sure you can't either," Barney went on. "We need someone to fight for Mazono. Someone who would show these scumbags that they can't just break rules with impunity."

Thoughts that Barney had been struggling to suppress broke free and rose to the surface. He strode to the windows, which offered him a panoramic view of the city. "The city needs someone like the Judge."

"I agree," Johnny replied. An idea began taking shape in his head. It might be crazy, but drastic times called for drastic measures.

These were indeed drastic times.

He was in the garden, and the scene played before him yet again. She lay on the ground, pleading.

"Help me, Johnny," she sobbed, as the masked man in ragged clothes raised a blade to her chin. Her face was pale with fear, the terror in her eyes palpable, as she stared at Johnny, willing him to do something. To save her from this monster. "Help me, Johnny."

He tried to move, but his body betrayed him. "Arrrrgh!" he grunted.

Suddenly, he was cradling her bloodied body in his arms. Tears poured from her eyes, mixing with the streaming blood that spurted from her chest and covered the rest of her body, soaking her flowery dress.

"Why did you let me die, Johnny?" she asked quietly, as he shook with his sobs. "Why?"

A sharp pain rent his chest, and he felt his hands losing their grip on her. Then he drifted down into an endless void, the darkness mingled with the distant laughter of the killer, which enveloped him like a heavy cloak.

"Why did you let me die, Johnny?"

Johnny woke up with a start, drenched with sweat, his heart pounding from fear. It took some time for his breathing to level. It had seemed real, so real. He buried his head in his hands, the pain washing over him in short spasms. He took a quick look around and realized that he was in the basement.

"Johnny?" Familiar hands reached for him. "Another nightmare?"

"Yeah."

"And she always blames you?"

"It kills me, Barney, every fucking time. I was this close to saving her this time, y'know?"

"But you couldn't."

"No, I couldn't."

"This is a battle of the mind," Barney asserted, going in search for a glass of water. "Your mind is throwing tricks at you, and you need to fight it."

"With what?" Johnny asked, throwing his hands in the air in exasperation. "I've tried everything."

Barney handed his friend the glass of water, watching him guzzle it.

"We make ourselves better," Barney said.

"How?"

"Training. If we are really going to do this, we have to do it right."

"This is the dumbest thing we've ever done, Barney."

"I know," Barney smiled, walking away from him, in search of the lights. "But I'm fresh out of solutions, and we're both sick of sitting on the sidelines. Get up, we have work to do."

Nikki stood next to Agent Zbysko beside the stainless-steel examination table in the basement morgue. She noted the pathologist's care not to disturb the shoulder-blade skin they'd cut to release the body from the wall.

The victim was a twenty-one-year-old named Lauren Fraser. She had recently accepted a position to work for the Mayor. Her name had surfaced when the lab ran her prints through the Automated Fingerprint Identification System (AFIS). The ever-expanding database now included anyone who'd applied for a passport, which Lauren had done before taking a recent trip.

Wearing a plastic face shield, Kim worked calmly as she examined the woman's body. Belying her delicate appearance, Kim was as comfortable dipping her hand into a bloody gunshot wound as peeling back the layers of society's skin with a well-placed question.

Nikki turned her attention back to the body. The skin was pale, translucent, showing the blue veins beneath. The victim lay supine, looking like a dressmaker's dummy, displaying perfectly formed breasts, a flat stomach, and well-defined hips. While affixed to the wall, her flesh had settled over her bones and given her a less emaciated appearance. On her back, however, she looked gaunt.

The victim's eyes stared up at the ceiling, blue but lifeless. Her heavy makeup was now obvious under bright lights in the morgue. The eyeliner and eye shadow had been carefully applied, evidence of a steady, experienced hand. Was the killer a cosmetologist? Or a drag queen, even? Nikki could barely make out vertical streaks running down from the corners of her eyes and ruining the perfect surface, as if poor Lauren had cried before the final application.

"… drugs in her system," Kim was saying. "Benzodiazepine, the same psychoactive sedative he's used before. More than enough to make her susceptible to suggestion."

"No sign of sexual contact?" Zbysko said.

"None."

Nikki caught Walt's sharp look. "That doesn't mean this wasn't a sexual act," she interjected.

He offered her a slight nod.

"Everything's as it was with the others, except for this." Kim traced her finger down to the victim's right heel. "This is what's new."

She picked up a small roll of bloody paper, maybe two inches long, and held it up between her thumb and forefinger. "This time he left this in the wound."

Zbysko stepped forward. "Writing?"

"I can see some markings, yes. But I haven't unrolled it yet. I thought you would want a look before I sent it up to the lab."

Walt's face paled.

The killer had left them a message.

Special Agent Barkley sat against the edge of the secretary desk on the conference room's north end and gazed at the rest of the team with brown, glassy eyes, hands folded beneath his chin. Nikki leaned against the wall, arms crossed, fixated on the enlarged photograph of the Slayer's note on the screen. Two other agents, McGough and Rodgers, lounged in chairs, their focus divided between the note and the other team members. Agent Zbysko began pacing.

"So, this is it," Barkley said. "We have us a certified whacko. A freaking lunatic from some funny barn who's out there poking holes in women to make a point." He looked around with a bemused look. "No pun intended, of course."

McGough and Rodgers guffawed, just as Nikki shot Barkley a sharp look. "I wouldn't put it like - "

"Spare me the psychobabble." He stood and shoved his hands into his pockets. "If this isn't certified crazy, I don't know what is."

"On balance, most pattern killers are mentally stable," Nikki said. "They are well-educated, financially stable, often good-looking, seemingly well-adjusted people. Unlike mass murderers, whose delusions feed beliefs of supremacy, serial killers act for personal gain or revenge. They do so in a calculated, thoughtful way. Hardly your standard lunatic."

"Read his note." Barkley frowned and jabbed his sharp, dimpled chin in the direction of the screen. "Any idiot can see that this religious nutcase slobbers on himself. You're saying you see something different?"

Nikki's face reddened, but she didn't point out the man's blunder in essentially calling himself an idiot. She looked at the screen.

The note was written in black lettering, with a fine ballpoint pen. The two-by-three-inch piece of white paper had been cut using a straightedge, then was folded several times before being rolled and inserted into the hole in Lauren's heel, at least several days after it had been written.

Walt read the poem again.

The Beauty Eden is Lost

Where intelligence does center

I came to her, and she smashed thy Serpent's head

I searched and found the final and beautiful

She will rest in my Serpent's hole

And I will live again.

"This imbecile is out of his fucking mind," Barclay spat.

Walt regarded the man. "I'm sorry, Jim, but I don't see an imbecile."

Barkley raised a brow and pulled out a chair to sit in.

"Is that right? Well, please…" He opened his palm in invitation. "Fill us in."

Nikki shifted her gaze to the dark window, struggling to hide her frustration.

"I think Nikki's assessment is right," Walt explained. "We're dealing with a highly intelligent individual who knows exactly what he's doing within the context of his world."

"Just because he knows how to clean up after himself doesn't mean he's not barking mad."

"No," Nikki interjected, "but even if he is suffering from psychosis, it doesn't mean he's an animal."

"I see motivation and intention," Zbysko continued, nodding at the note on the screen. "It would be a significant mistake not to assume the author knew exactly what he was writing and why he was writing it."

"You're saying he's broadcasting his next move," Barkley said, glancing back at the note. "How so?"

"Assume with me that this was written by a scholar; a poet with the intelligence of Hemingway. And written for our benefit."

"I realize that. But go with me. What's he saying?"

"The beauty of Eden is lost," Nikki read. "The fall of innocence."

Barkley closed his eyes momentarily in a show of impatience. "Fine. Something less obvious."

Zbysko nodded at Nikki. She exchanged an inquisitive look with him, nodded her appreciation, and looked up at the screen.

"He's saying that where once beauty, innocence, and intelligence were found, this Eden, it's now lost. The serpent—read evil or the devil—is responsible. Not sure about the third line—'I came to her, and she smashed thy Serpent's head.' Doesn't make sense to me," Nikki finished.

She glanced at Walt.

"Motivation," Walt said. "He, the serpent, destroyed beauty but was wounded in the process. He's upset. Go on."

Nikki nodded. "I can go with that. The last three lines seem straightforward. The killer is a replacement for the beautiful one who fell so that the killer can live again."

"He's looking for a wife," Walt said. "A new Eve."

"And this helps us how?" Rodgers asked.

Barkley ignored him entirely, having stood to pace. "Okay, I'm with you. Tell me more."

Walt walked behind the conference table, keeping his eyes fixed on the words written in the killer's hand. He could see it all.

Neatly arranged. Perfectly ordered. A pen poised over the paper just so, while the words he had recited to himself a thousand times flowed through his mind, sung by a choir, a chorus in a symphony. A requiem that thundered the truth, demanding to be heard.

Now such truth was reduced to mere words on a simple piece of white paper, for his greatest enemies to see. It was like being stripped naked, both terrifying and thrilling at once. The killer was coming out. His whole life was here, on this piece of paper.

He cleared his throat. "His killings are ritualistic, leading him to life. He's not doing it out of anger. None of the crime scenes have shown signs of rage."

Walt reviewed the history in his mind. Local authorities had found the first victim a year ago in a barn just south of the city. Serena Barker had been twenty-three, and the police had assumed her to be a victim of satanic ritual.

The Mazono Special Investigations office hadn't been engaged until the second body was found sixty miles northeast of Mazono, in an apartment near the plains cattle town of Greeley. Karen Neely, twenty-four. Again, carefully preserved, nearly flawless in her final presentation. Walt had been assigned the case and immediately requested copies of the file from Grand Junction. A studious detective had meticulously documented the case.

There was little doubt that they had a serial killer on their hands.

The Slayer killed his third woman a month later in Parker, south of Mazono. Julia Paxton was twenty-one and had been found less than eight hours after her death, a vision of twisted beauty glued to the wall of a remote barn.

Last, there had been April Smith, twenty-five, who was killed in Mazono Gardens. She wasn't preserved like the others and was killed on the spot.

All women under the age of twenty-six. All exceptionally beautiful. As of yet, only one murder had garnered mainstream publicity — that of Julia Paxton, who was a well-known model. Other than the distinctive circumstances of death, they could determine no connection among the women.

As for the killer, recovered evidence from the previous scenes put him at 180 to 200 pounds based on the depth of his shoe indentations in soil.

No DNA to run through CODIS — the Combined DNA Index System. No hair or cell samples. No saliva, blood, semen, or latent prints tied to the killer.

He was essentially a ghost.

"His motivation is in finding life," Walt continued, "not in delivering death. He believes he's leading the women into life."

Barkley stared at him. "You see, now there's where my psycho-nutcase warning bells start going crazy. Forgive me if I don't see torturing and killing someone 'into life' as anything less than barking mad."

"Psychotic, maybe," Nikki said. "Mentally ill, maybe. But not necessarily less intelligent than any of us. The direct link between psychosis and intelligence is well documented in some subjects. We should assume that the Slayer is more intelligent than anyone in this room. If we don't, we risk seriously underestimating him."

"That's your profile? Our man's a genius?"

She hesitated. "Yes."

Barkley crossed his arms and settled back against the desk. "Okay, I'll let you go with that."

"There's more," Walt said. "He wants us to know he's going after beautiful women. That much is unmistakable in his writing. He wants us to look for a supremely intelligent person who has a penchant for killing beautiful women because he's been jilted by one. Yet in reality, that's not the case. Sound right to you, Nikki?"

Her blue eyes widened. She nodded, lost in thought. "Eerily right."

Barkley drummed his fingers on the desk. "Okay, so we play his game his way. We look for the most beautiful women in and around Mazono."

"That's what he wants us to do," McGough said.

"I'm open to suggestions," Walt said. "In the absence of any, we keep him engaged, even if it means playing things his way. Keep it under wraps. We don't need everyone who thinks they're decent-looking in a panic. Any tire tracks lifted at the shack scene?"

"None," said McGough.

"Other evidence processed?" Walt questioned.

"So far he's clean," McGough said. "The fresh hair, bodily fluids, and fingerprints match the victim. There were three other hair samples and we're running them now. Could be from anyone messing around in there."

Barkley nodded at McGough and glanced at the others. "Any other ideas?"

Nikki shifted off the wall again and paced. "You want to play his way, start with all known cases of mental illness in the state."

"So now he's a whacko again?" Barkley said.

"You're not listening. Again, being a genius and mentally ill are not mutually exclusive," Nikki explained.

"But you're willing to concede that he could be nuts," Barkley persisted.

She breathed out slowly. "I think our guy could be deeply disturbed, just not 'nuts.' Maybe psychotic and delusional, maybe suffering from acute schizophrenia, but he doesn't slobber."

Barkley frowned. "Then until we learn differently, we assume he's both mentally ill and a genius. Fair enough?"

She nodded. "The ones that aren't complete loners tend to congregate on the internet, in psychiatrists' offices, psychiatric wards. It's a starting point."

"As of now, we start looking for records of any anomalies or patterns in mental health facilities, residential care homes, whatever." Barkley turned quickly to Zbysko. "Pull whatever resources you need, cross-check what we know of the Slayer against the files of every known psycho released from any facility in the last" — he looked at Nikki — "ten years?"

"Too many cases. Mental illness is more widespread than you think. Nearly seven hundred thousand mentally ill are jailed each year in this country. Start with a year."

Barkley looked stunned. Walt found it odd that the man wasn't already familiar with this statistic. "God help us all." He glanced up at the wall clock, which was closing in on ten. "A year then. I have to go."

Zbysko spoke before the man could move. "We should also assume he intends to kill one more woman. It appears he may have found his next, and possibly final, target."

That brought a pause.

"It fits," said Walt. He pushed on quickly, "Based on his previous behavior, it's impossible to determine a timeline with him. However, if he is down to a final target, he may murder another woman within days. If it takes him a few days to prep the kill, then he's likely already engaged. It's a short cycle for a pattern killer who kills to satisfy compulsion. But our guy's method is based on reason, not raw compulsion."

The others stared at him, arms crossed.

"Okay. I gotta go." Barkley grabbed his cell phone and walked toward the door. "We assume our guy is out there now, outwitting us morons, stalking a beautiful woman he intends to kill in the next few days." He turned back at the door. "For the love of all that is holy, stop him."

Their training began in the basement of Johnny's father's building.

Barney decided that the first thing that Johnny would have to do was hone his body to the peak of physical fitness and maximum strength. Johnny would have called Barney a sadist, but Barney trained by Johnny's side every inch of the way.

The first instrument of torture was the salmon ladder. Not only was Johnny to do chin-ups on it, but after each chin-up, he needed to throw the bar up six inches to the next notch, using only his body's momentum. Each chin-up was done one notch higher on the ladder. Rinse and repeat until Johnny swore he was near death.

Next came a contraption that secured Johnny's feet to the ceiling, aptly named, by Johnny, the upside-down torment device. Hanging from it, he'd pull his body upward into sit-ups and crunches, twisting and straining until every muscle screamed.

As if that wasn't enough, there was the rope. To start, he climbed it hand over hand with it flung over one shoulder so that he couldn't assist with his legs. Eventually, he climbed it while holding his legs at a ninety-degree angle to his body and pointing toward the ceiling.

Then there were the torture cables. They ran through pulleys connected to weights heavier than transport trucks. Johnny would work with them to Barney's directions, targeting one muscle at a time until his body burned as if on fire.

Last but not least was the 'death trap,' a machine with metal blades that whirled round and round on the bottom, and round and round on the top. When Johnny was in it, his objective was to survive in one piece by avoiding the two sets of spinning blades, jumping over one and ducking under the other, over and over, as the speed increased to a breathless whir and Johnny's heart rate hit maximum levels.

Johnny did these exercises, and more, day in and day out, until finally Barney was satisfied and moved Johnny's training to the next stage. Combat training. Johnny began by fighting an apparatus with protrusions that looked like arms and legs and emulated an opponent's kicks and punches.

After mastering that beast, Johnny and Barney fought with one another under the guidance of his old trainer. Once their technique had reached satisfactory levels, they fought with metal pipes. Then knives. Then they fought without weapons, turning their arms and legs into their weapons.

Next came the arrow training. This started very simply with Barney throwing a tennis ball into the air and Johnny shooting an arrow at it. And missing. Again, and again.

Tonight, they were in the basement again. A dim bulb illuminated the space. In the middle of the room, Barney and Johnny faced one another, fists drawn up, eyes trained upon each other. For months they had trained here, suffering through grueling workouts and fighting hand-to-hand.

The men circled each other, each looking for the other's weak point. Finally, Johnny made the first move, feigning a jab with his left fist, before swiftly hitting Barney in the stomach with his right.

Barney stumbled back, and that was all the time it took for Johnny to drop him to the floor with a double leg takedown before smoothly transitioning into a chokehold. Barney tapped out immediately. He lay there for a while, breathing heavily. "No matter what I do, I always end up tapping out. Maybe you should've gone pro after all."

Johnny shrugged and extended an arm to his friend. "I saw my dad live that lifestyle. I'm glad I passed on it," he said.

Barney nodded, accepted the hand that was offered, and allowed his friend to pull him to his feet.

"This will be a lot wor—" Johnny replied. Before he could finish his sentence, he was distracted by a news bulletin on the television, which had been muted in the course of their fight. Frowning, he picked up a remote and restored the sound.

"…*the body of a young woman was found in an alley in the Backstreets. Investigation is still ongoing as to the identity of the woman, but anonymous sources suggest that it might be Lauren Fraser, aged twenty-three, who was reported missing a few days ago. The police insist that they are on top of the situation and advise citizens not to panic.*"

"On top of the situation, my ass," Johnny said bitterly. "Confused and overwhelmed is more like it." He unhooked the weighted vest he had been wearing and angrily strode to the small refrigerator in the corner. Taking out a bottle of water, he downed it instantly.

Barney shook his head. "Pathetic."

"They have no clue," Johnny said, wiping his mouth. "Like Walbrick pointed out, they are underpaid, and understaffed. Not to mention unqualified. They need help."

With that, he put the bottle on the table. "It's time for the next level."

Johnny had moved gradually from that first lobbed tennis ball, to a bag filled with them, connected to a pipe that shot the balls out at dizzying speed. Johnny stood in front of the contraption and tried to shoot an arrow through the flying balls, pinning them to the wall.

At first, the speed had been too fast for Johnny to even target, but over time his reflexes improved, and his accuracy followed. Even Barney had seemed impressed.

Johnny now walked to a table on which a quiver filled with arrows was resting, picked it up, and carried it by its shoulder strap.

"Are you ready?" Barney asked.

He nodded.

Barney walked over to a small laptop and in a quick series of events, different mechanized targets jumped out at Johnny, nearly simultaneously. For the next few minutes, Johnny ran, jumped over obstacles, dodged heavy objects thrown at him, and shot at moving targets until he was safely on the other side of the room, breathing hard. He looked over at Barney. "Well?"

"New record," Barney said, examining the screen. "It took you only two minutes to get through the course. Your reflexes are sharper, and you are faster. Your aim, as usual, was top notch." He looked up thoughtfully. "This is good."

Barney stalked to where the gear was and placed his hand on the quiver, now back on the table. "But it's not enough."

"You're right, it's not. I need to be out there on the streets, making sure that bastard pays."

Barney sighed. "This is bigger than just the Slayer," he said. "We've been over this. We can't truly make a difference by taking down one man. All these other thugs aren't just going to go away. The system is broken. We can be the ones to fix it."

"As long as that piece of shit gets what's coming to him," Johnny replied. After a brief silence, he added, "It's about time we find out what I'm able to do."

"We need to play this smart, Johnny. You're a lot more skilled than your average thug, but the Slayer is something else entirely. We have to be absolutely certain you're ready for anything and everything that comes your way."

"Only one way to do that." Johnny folded his hands and leaned against the table, tension visible in his stance. "Barney," he said pleadingly. "I need you for this to work. Help me. Just a test run. No amount of training can prepare me for what the streets have to offer. It's too clean. If I'm to succeed at this, I need to get out there. You know I do, Barney."

Barney sighed and looked away.

"Barney," Johnny said, as the latter bent over the computer. "We need to act now. We need to start some trial runs. Not here, not in a controlled environment. I need to go out into the streets. There's no other way to find out how the streets work. Barney," he continued, his voice low and earnest, "we need to take action now. People are dying. And he's still out there."

Barney straightened up and looked into his friend's eyes. "Okay," he finally said. "Let's do this."

For the first time in what felt like ages, Johnny smiled.

"So far," Barney began, "we've been able to monitor the criminal activities in this corner of the city." He walked to a table whose surface was littered with tech.

Earlier, they'd spent a day searching for anything useful to their cause, and had discovered an abandoned police radio, which Barney quickly repaired.

Now, Barney looked at his friend.

"If you're going to go on the streets, you'll need something to hide your identity."

"What, like a costume?" Johnny asked. "I have a dark hoodie that should do the trick. That and a ski mask should be fine."

Barney shook his head.

"You'll need better than that. You need clothing that'll not only protect your identity: it'll also give you a new one. Once you put it on, you'll no longer be Johnny Carmichael. When you don the costume, you're gonna be someone else. You'll be…" and here he paused, thinking. After a while, he said, "You also need a name."

Johnny pulled out a chair and straddled it. "I don't need a name, Barney. I don't need to reinvent myself or anything like that. I only need to go out and clean up the streets. That's what the Judge did. He never came out calling himself that." Then an idea came to Johnny, and he brightened. "You can call me the Cleaner."

"Sounds like a nickname you'd give a wrestler," Barney remarked wearily. "Surely you can do better than that."

Johnny was quiet for awhile as he considered it. Then he rolled his eyes and scoffed again. "Let's just get to it, Barney. We'll worry about names later.

Let's get back to the issue of clothing. I saw the look on your face when I suggested what I have to wear. What do you have in mind?"

Barney rubbed his jaw. "I think I have an idea…"

He picked up the police radio and turned it on.

The next evening, the police radio crackled to life and announced a double homicide downtown. A man and his wife had just been murdered. The dispatcher was calling the nearest available policemen to the scene. Johnny listened to the radio with a grim look on his face. The woman's ring was missing. This could be him. The Slayer.

The downtown Mazono area was in chaos. Police sirens filled the air, which was thick with tension and fear. People who lived in the area were watching the whole scenario from behind the curtains of their homes.

Detective Dusty Roenega's face was grim as he examined the spectacle before him. From all appearances, both the man and the woman were young, and seemed to be newlyweds. The framed picture on their mantle of the man in a suit and the woman in a wedding gown looked new. He gritted his teeth and rubbed a hand through his hair in frustration.

One of the neighbors had called the police immediately after they heard the screams. The first squad car got to the scene a long twenty minutes after the call came in, because the force was spread so thin. Upon arrival, the officers had caught sight of a man running away from the scene and had immediately gone after him, but he'd gotten away, disappearing into the shadows.

Upon hearing the details, Roenega felt the color drain from his face. A young woman being stabbed to death and something valuable missing. He knew this M.O. He again ran a hand through his unkempt hair, frustrated and angry. *This damn city.* Being a veteran on the police force had not rendered him immune to feelings of anger each time a crime like this was committed. *I'm damn well going to catch this monster!*

He surveyed the crime scene in front of him. Both of the victims had been stabbed in the heart. A ring was missing. This had to be the Slayer. Though his gut told him that he was missing something: something right under his nose. Having learned to trust his instincts, he stood in the middle of the room and let his eyes go over everything, taking little mental notes as he did so.

The bodies weren't displayed in the same manner as the others. Every previous Slayer kill had a single female victim displayed with her body contorted to form a "Y" shape, with a knife plunged into her heart. All except that of the lawyer, where there had been multiple female victims. That killing had been attributed to the Slayer because of the way the body had been laid out at the base of the statue, the knife through the victim's heart, and the stolen necklace.

This time, the bodies were not displayed in any manner. Unlike those that were nailed in a "Y" shape onto a wall, or the lawyer who was draped in a "Y" shape beneath the statue of an angel, this time the female laid crumpled across the legs of the male victim, as if she had fallen there that way. This killing didn't feel right.

The Slayer had had some time to display the body, so that hadn't been the issue. Why hadn't he displayed her? Come to think of it, had the Slayer ever killed a man before? Also, tonight the killer had barely escaped as the cops arrived. The Slayer had only been seen once before, and that had been long before police arrived at the scene. Had he really been clumsy enough to nearly get caught tonight? This wasn't adding up.

At that point, the medical examiner, a balding man who was not pleased to be here in the freezing night, approached Roenega. The information he had to share was not particularly helpful. It was already rather obvious that they had been stabbed multiple times a little earlier that night. The medical examiner said he would autopsy the bodies in the morning and left the room.

Policemen swarmed like bees all over the house, dusting for fingerprints, taking pictures, gathering evidence. Roenega approached one of them and asked if anybody had come across a diamond ring. No one had found one. Sooner or later, a regular thief would try to sell it, hoping to make some quick cash. "You won't get away with this," muttered Roenega under his breath.

On a roof opposite the house, Johnny watched and waited, trying to get a feel for what was happening. He watched through binoculars as the bodies were loaded into an ambulance and driven away. He saw Detective Roenega come out of the house with his partner. After jumping down from the roof, he hurried closer, in order to hear what they were saying. He slipped behind a tree where he could see them, but they wouldn't spot him.

"Tell the press it was a botched burglary," Roenega was saying. "They walked in on the thief, and he killed them. We don't need to induce any more panic across this damn city. No need for Zbysko on this one."

Johnny leaned back on his haunches and thought. A robbery gone wrong? No, this was a deliberate murder. He looked at Roenega. The other man said something too low for Johnny to decipher.

"Yes, we've gone through the whole house," Roenega said. "Hopefully, we'll nail this guy. I think we're looking at a Slayer copycat."

Johnny was intrigued. *Now, that's news.* He focused on Roenega again.

"The perp stole a diamond ring," Roenega said to his partner. "The previous victims were also stabbed through the heart and had something stolen from them. Those were the only details that we released to the press." He cleared his throat. "We never described how the victims were displayed. The couple here appear to have simply been left where he killed them, and there is nowhere near the level of precision in the stabbings as there's been in the past cases. Whoever did this was sloppy: we may have found a print on the table. If we're lucky, he'll try to pawn off the ring."

The other man turned toward Johnny, appearing to gaze into the night. "So, you're telling me we may need to enlist those of our friends in the Backstreets to gather further details. I'll let them know this whole business is meant to look like the work of the Slayer."

Johnny pondered his next move. It didn't take long for him to come up with an answer. He left his hiding spot and vanished into the darkness. This was one killer that wouldn't get away.

The murderer felt on top of the world. It was a powerful feeling knowing he could command such fear. The buzz from forcing his knife into those people was unlike any other he had experienced.

He smiled as he remembered the diamond ring he'd pulled from the dead woman's finger. Hopefully, he'd be able to sell it for big bucks. With luck, he'd have enough to send to his loser sister, and plenty left over to stock up on coke. The best part was that he was home free in regard to getting caught. He'd staged it to look like the Slayer had committed the crime. No one would ever come looking for him. He smiled. Yes, life was good.

The killer arrived at Charlie's Bar, and went in. He swaggered up to the bar and ordered a beer.

"How's it goin' Charlie? Packed house tonight, eh?" he said.

"Here ya go Shawn," Charlie replied, passing him his beer.

Beer in hand, Shawn turned and assessed the crowd. Right up front was a table openly displaying some handguns. Over to the left, he saw two uniformed officers taking turns snorting a substance off the counter they stood by. To the right sat Tyrone McClain and his crew. That wasn't someone to get into it with. Other groups around the bar were roaring incoherent sentences at each other and laughing.

Then there were the DeMarco brothers in the back left corner. They were the people he needed to talk to. He picked up his beer and approached their table. Somewhere in the back of the bar, a hooded figure sat quietly, nursing a beer.

Nobody had paid any attention to the hooded man when he came in because the bar was filled with similarly hooded figures. So nobody paid any attention to Johnny in the back. With nobody watching him, it was easy for him to observe everything that was going on in here.

Johnny knew this would be his best chance to find the killer, who was likely in here looking for a buyer for the stolen ring. Because Johnny was not with the police, he didn't have to follow their rules or respect their agreement with Charlie. He shifted uncomfortably and took a sip of his beer, hoping nobody noticed his movement. His clothes were restrictive, and boiling hot. Still, he kept a sharp eye out.

Johnny had a feeling the killer would come here tonight. If an amateur, he would want to get the ring off his hands as soon as possible. So when the youth with the flushed cheeks and shifty eyes came in, Johnny zeroed in on him. The young man betrayed all the signs of being high. More than that, there was something about him…his wide toothy grin and puffed out chest were rubbing Johnny the wrong way.

He watched as the man went straight to the bar, got a beer, and surveyed the crowd, then approached Tony DeMarco and his brothers. Johnny's focus narrowed. He knew all about the DeMarcos. If this goon were looking to sell a diamond ring, they would be the ones he'd approach. Johnny took a sip of his beer and continued to surreptitiously watch the young man.

As expected, the killer sauntered right to the table of the DeMarco brothers, who appeared to be engrossed in a card game. After a few words, it appeared he was invited to sit at the table, and a short period of deliberation followed. The young man waved his hands around while the other men just drank their beers and looked at him, occasionally getting a word in. The youth grew more agitated as the conversation went on. Finally, when the men sitting at the table stopped speaking and merely shrugged, he stood up and left the bar.

Johnny waited a few minutes before he left to go follow him.

Shawn was outraged. Eight hundred bucks! For a diamond ring! It had to be worth more than that! Those men were nothing but thieves, robbers! He had killed for that ring! That thought sobered him up briefly. He had hoped to get a few thousand for it, and now the DeMarco brothers were offering him eight hundred!

He gritted his teeth as he remembered the nonchalant look on their faces when he threatened to take the ring to a non-existent rival buyer who would give him more money for it. They knew he was lying, of course. Yes, there were others who dealt in stuff such as this, but none of them would accept the merchandise while it was still hot.

He let out his frustration in a stream of curses. He had no choice but to sell, and the DeMarco brothers knew that. He briefly considered holding on to the ring until the police hunt cooled down, but he knew that it would be too dangerous. Even if they thought it was the Slayer, he couldn't afford to still have the ring on him if they swarmed the place.

He swore again. He had told the DeMarco brothers that he was going to retrieve the ring from where he had hidden it. That was no lie: out of fear of running into the police and risking the ring being found on his person, he had chosen to leave it hidden beneath the floorboards under his bed. The DeMarcos did not have to worry about his lying to them; their reputation was such that only a person with absolutely no sense of self-preservation would do so.

Engrossed in his thoughts, he didn't notice that he was being followed. On he went, still making calculations about just how many drugs he could purchase with the amount he was offered. When he got to a dismal-looking apartment building, he let himself in. He grabbed the ring, muttering to himself all the while. He was being swindled, that was just it. Exploited, extorted.

He walked back outside, holding the ring in his hand. A movement penetrated his drug-addled mind, and he looked up, suddenly alert. What was that sound? He stood quietly, listening. When he heard nothing else, he walked on…until a blow doubled him over.

"Aaaaargh…" he moaned, coughing and sputtering. "Ahh, fuck!"

By reflex, his hands found his gun, and he shot blindly into the darkness.

The next thing he knew, he was being kicked into the wall. His head ricocheted off it and he dropped his gun, stunned.

What's happening? He tried to gain his bearings through a fog of confusion.

With his heart pounding, he dropped to his knees to scramble for his gun. As he looked around for his attacker, he heard the gun being kicked away.

"You're not who I was hoping to find, but you'll do," came a low, taunting voice.

The killer looked up to see a figure come into focus in the moonlight. Wearing a hood, the stranger stood with his whole body tensed and ready to attack again.

Jumping to his feet, Shawn roared, charging the figure headfirst. Johnny braced himself for the impact, then used the attacker's momentum to lift him up and throw him into a nearby fence.

The collision bounced Shawn onto his back. As he tried to regain his footing, the hooded figure pinned him down.

He reached into his pocket for his knife. He wouldn't go down easy!

His attempt to reach the knife was thwarted as the hooded figure neatly slid back Shawn's wrist, breaking his hold of the weapon. Johnny tossed the knife aside and smashed his fist into his victim's jaw.

"Awwww…" Shawn moaned in pain, still incensed. He wouldn't be cheated out of what was rightfully his!

Stumbling to his feet once more, he turned to face his assailant, who seemed to be waiting for him to get up.

"Come and get me," that taunting voice came again.

Shawn charged blindly again, throwing wild punches.

The restrictive material Johnny was wearing hindered his mobility. He dodged awkwardly, and Shawn's fist connected lightly with his ribs before Johnny retaliated with a punch to the stomach that winded his opponent.

As Shawn tried to catch his breath, an elbow came down on his head, busting it open, before a final punch knocked him out cold.

When Shawn came to that night, he was in the police station, his hands and legs bound by a rope, the incriminating diamond ring in his coat pocket. Detective Roenega watched as the bewildered youth was taken away in cuffs for questioning. Then he shook his head. It was starting again.

Meanwhile, in a basement not too far away, Johnny swore as he finally took his hoodie off.

"Damnit, Barney, I thought this was going to be him."

Barney calmly looked away from the computer where he had been watching Johnny's movements, and said, "Are you sure turning him in was the best idea? You could've finished him right there. One less criminal on the streets."

"Yeah, I know," Johnny replied, irritated. "But Barney, he was just a kid. Nineteen or twenty years old, tops. We didn't start this so I could kill people. Besides, we have to talk about this material: my mobility was seriously compromised."

"That's not what it sounded like to me," Barney replied dryly. He pointed to his headset. "It seemed like you were moving just fine."

Johnny rolled his eyes and removed the armor he was wearing. He could have sworn his whole body gave a sigh of relief as he got it off.

"He wouldn't have been able to lay a hand on me otherwise."

"You're right. You could've killed him. I'm still not sure you shouldn't have. But for the time being, we do have better things to worry about."

"Like I said, he was a kid. He just needed to be taught a lesson," Johnny replied. Though he couldn't get the mental image of the Slayer out of his head when he was fighting that kid. If he hadn't heard sirens, he didn't know what he would have done. He reminded himself the guy was just a desperate teen. He didn't deserve to die in the street, without a trial. Johnny took a swig of cool, refreshing water. Mazono was to blame for this.

"Johnny," Barney's voice was filled with concern and warning.

"Oh, knock it off, man. I got the guy, didn't I? He was too weak and too distracted to even put up a proper fight." Johnny walked over to a chest of drawers and got a t-shirt from the first drawer. "No challenge at all," he said, as he pulled it on.

"It won't always be that way," Barney replied.

"Yeah, I get it." Johnny picked up the water bottle and took another long swig. "Back to the costume. It's restrictive. The armor is uncomfortable, the hoodie is heavy…what material is it made from, asbestos?"

"You need the armor to protect you from bullets…"

"If I don't die from suffocation first," Johnny cut in. "Come on, Barney. There must be something better we can come up with. There has to be. This is unsustainable."

"And your quiver?" Barney asked. "Did you have any problems with it?"

Johnny looked to where his bow and quiver lay on the table. "It wasn't exactly handy," he replied. "I had to hide it behind some dumpsters when I went into Charlie's. Also, I can barely see with that hoodie on. It was bad enough that it was dark out; the hoodie distorted my vision."

Barney had been writing everything down on a notepad. "Okay, that's good to know," he said. "This was our first go at it, so it was never going to be perfect. I'll get to work on this."

"Thank you," Johnny said, sitting on the edge of the table. "So, you've heard my observations. What are yours?"

"Your voice…." Barney remarked.

"What?"

"You spoke at various times."

"Yes, I did. I wanted to rile the bastard up."

"Did you consider that he might recognize your voice?"

Johnny fell silent.

"Of course you didn't. I'll come up with something to take care of that. We lucked out that you didn't face the real Slayer today. We have some kinks we need to fix. Other than that, tonight's outing was rather cut and dried. Oh, but next time try not to have any alcohol on a mission."

"Probably a good idea," Johnny agreed, looking out the window.

So it's begun, he thought. *This is for you, April.*

The Backstreets were known for the influx of gangs that prowled and pillaged from unsuspecting inhabitants, leaving bullet shells and crimson in their wake, and for the drug dealing menace that often enveloped the area. Now a dangerous killer lurked in the shadows, roaming the streets when the sun went to sleep, and the clubhouses woke with boisterous activities. Residents spoke of him only in whispers, behind the safety of locked doors and windows.

The Mazono Police Department had been unable to track this killer, who vanished from each crime scene before police had a fighting chance to tail him.

Detectives Jason Walbrick and Dusty Roenega swiftly wrapped up cases that fit into the killer's modus operandi: a bloodied female victim, her body posed to form a "Y," an item of the victim's stolen, and finally, a knife lodged in her heart.

No autopsy or coroner's report shed further light in any way. Darkness masked the psychopath, as his reputation grew more sinister with each new unsolved kill.

Every coroner's report read the same: it almost seemed as if the coroner simply made copies of the same report for all the brazen kills. *Why bother wasting quality time looking for the real-life version of Waldo?*

The cases were a chore, and because the detectives saw the cases as a dead-end, they saw nothing amiss in shelving the unsolved cases and calling it a day. Roenega knew he couldn't waste departmental resources on these cases, and so he set out on his own, on his own time, to figure these killings out.

The lonesome serial killer hadn't always been this brash, this brutish, or this vicious-looking.

The world is filled with light. But with light comes darkness.

Back in the *good ol' days*, when the clouds hovering above Mazono skies held opportunities, the handsome Tomas Creed was a popular brand amongst circus performers and spectators alike. Tomas was the headliner for Mr. Hickenbottom's Moving Circus — a circus whose performers were known for their aerial manoeuvres and death-defying stunts. An incredible success story, he rose from poverty to become a star before the age of eighteen. The only remainder of his previous life was a collection of battered, life-size dolls his family had owned before their passing. He cherished them.

In the heat of the moment, when spirits were high, the circus would announce him. He would enter bearing knives, bow in obeisance to the spectators — it was something he'd learned from the greats before him — and would start throwing the knives at different strategically-placed targets located throughout the tent. His deft knife-throwing fired up the spectators with excitement.

However, in time, the audience's excitement waned, and boos were elicited whenever he, or any other circus performer, failed to provide something new. On some days, rotten fruit connected with performers' faces, ruining their routines and flustering them. Tomas Creed was no exception.

Soon, Mr. Hickenbottom's Moving Circus was swimming in debt, and on the verge of folding up. The end seemed inevitable: most of the top performers ran off to set up solo acts on their own from the proceeds they'd been saving. Creed remained for one reason: Yasmin.

Yasmin was the elder of Mr. Hickenbottom's two children. She was as beautiful as the doll collection Tomas Creed's family had left him. At times, he wished she were one of the dolls so he could worship her forever. There was a way Creed felt whenever she entered a room in her slow, slick manner, her glowing hair swaying around her, her skin smooth and soft as the silk she wore. Her face held a smile that literally sucked the life out of him. He'd never felt that way about other lays he had. It surprised him when he found out she felt the same way about him, too.

They were deeply in love, Creed and Yasmin, and even though he hinted at running away from her father and the circus, she never budged. Unwavering loyalty to her father and family were paramount to her. Her brother, Elias, whose famed archery act had once been the main event of the circus, was their biggest detractor. He'd taken aim at Creed on numerous occasions after finding out about Creed's relationship with his sister. So, Creed stayed behind and brainstormed ideas to revive the circus.

Creed's frustration built as he attempted to return prestige to the show. He spent much time alone, sitting with his collection, admiring them, as he tried to find a way to save the circus. Then one day as he cleaned his collection of knives, an idea struck him like a moving train. When he discussed it with Yasmin, she wasn't keen on it, so in his spare time he worked on it alone.

Two months later, he talked Mr. Hickenbottom into allowing his new act into the show. From day one, it was a certified success. Residents of Mazono started milling in huge numbers to ogle at the man who could throw knives from a distance at the human dolls pinned to a wooden platform. They watched in awe as the knives swirled and made a sickening thunk on the board, dangerously pinning the outlines of his targets.

News travels fast, and competing papers fought to get a story on the 20th-century wonder.

However, those who do not learn from the past are doomed to repeat it. The thrill of his new act gradually waned; knife throwing at a dress-up doll wasn't sustaining viewers' attention. Creed needed to do more, to push the limits and write his story in the sands of time. Like an icon. Like a legend.

He approached Yasmin again, and this time she succumbed to his proposal for a new act. After watching him succeed time and time again with the dolls, despite her initial doubts, she grew to trust him. They lay out together one night under the City's Angel in Mazono Gardens. He would never forget that night. A night filled with fiery moments of passion.

The next day, against the wishes of her brother, Yasmin was blindfolded and chained to the same wooden board Creed had been using for the dolls. The knives he threw pegged dangerously close to his beloved's still frame without so much as scraping her dress.

Actual lives being on the line kept the dollar bills flowing to Hickenbottom for a relatively long period of time. Creed, and his now-fiancée, Yasmin, were recipients of many accolades and were worth more money than they had ever imagined possible. Creed, however, wasn't satisfied. The drive to do more drove him mad. He spent sleepless nights devising new plans to stun the world and become a legend.

When Creed told Yasmin of a new stunt he wanted them to try out, she didn't object as she had done before. She had found out that she felt remarkably safe with him, and she trusted him totally, even with her greatest gift: her life.

Again, her brother voiced strong concerns against this stunt, but he had no say in the matter according to Yasmin. She knew what she was getting into, so who was he to object?

The practices of this latest stunt were held behind closed doors and with an intensity like never before. It was perfect.

The big day arrived, and while every spectator in the circus tent was expecting to be at least mildly thrilled by the performers, the unexpected happened.

A set of circus workers had carried a sophisticated circular wooden platform on the stage and affixed it tightly. Soon after, Yasmin appeared on the stage — beautiful as ever — bowing to teeming spectators, and standing close to the circular object.

Yasmin had given Tomas her engagement ring to hold for good luck. Before he made his way to center stage to join her, Elias pulled Creed aside. "If you harm my sister, I will kill you." His gaze fell towards the quiver sitting in the corner. Tomas paid him no mind.

The drums rolled when Tomas Creed appeared with a tray containing his vast assortment of knives. He walked the ramp slowly, feeding off the energy from the screams of the spectators.

When he kissed the lips of his fiancée in front of a live audience, the tent vibrated. After a series of waves and bows, he proceeded to tie her spread-eagled on the platform, and tapped on a switch by the side. The platform began to rotate slowly, Yasmin pinned.

A pregnant silence hung in the air, save for the half-creaking, half-whistling sound the platform made as it rotated. He peered over his shoulder to take a mocking glance at Elias.

When the first knife fastened close to Yasmin's hip, an inch's breath from her skin, the spectators yelled in excitement. The thrill was overwhelming. Creed saw, and he knew he had the crowd eating from the palm of his hand.

He drew his hands on his lips, and the crowd went silent. The second blade flew from his grasp, swirled in an arc and stuck to close to his bride-to-be's ear. An ensuing scream followed.

The third. The fourth. The eighth. The ninth. All blades lodged safely on the platform without harming the radiant, rotating figure of Yasmin.

There was just one blade left. The screams from the crowd had reached a fevered decibel. The newscasters airing the live show were speaking animatedly into the cameras facing them. Away from the stage, Mr. Hickenbottom was smiling as another metaphorical truckload of cash was delivered to his office. His soon to be son-in-law was, as Hickenbottom had always dreamed, an entertainment *god*.

Tomas Creed juggled the last blade between his palms. With every toss caught, the crowd grew more electrified.

"Throw it! Throw it!" They screamed, pumping fists into the air all around the tent.

His whole life then flashed in bits before him, as the knife flew out of his hand, swirling in the air. How far he had come, from the days of his childhood, from living on scraps and pillaging for necessities in trash cans, from how he'd arrived home one day to meet the lifeless bodies of his parents who had overdosed on narcotics, how authorities had seized everything from his home except the dolls, how he'd fled from various foster care homes without a trace — breaking free from the shackles of his regulated life, till he found himself in Mr. Hickenbottom's Moving Circus.

Legends are made of this. Only a fool could doubt me. This is my chance to become immortal. A god.

The knife struck.

The hall fell silent, the suspense palpable in their faces. It had happened so fast, it was hard to process.

The last knife found a safe haven lodged in Yasmin's chest, piercing her heart. Her body twitched, her mouth flew open, trying to speak, but the light left her eyes before she could say a word. Her body pulsed once and stilled.

Before the horrific reality dawned on the crowd, Creed's natural flight response kicked in. He dashed out of the tent, escaping to the nearby woods, and disappeared. In mere moments, Elias had gathered his quiver to strike down the murderer but it was too late. He was gone. An all-out APB was placed on Creed. The papers tagged the gory event: *The Death of The Circus.*

Mr. Hickenbottom and his son spent their vast fortune on private investigators, trying to locate Creed, but it was to no avail. It was as though he'd disappeared from the face of the earth. After a few years of endless investigation and false leads, the police gave up on the search for Creed. The private investigators concluded that he might be dead, killed by a wild beast, even. But they were all wrong.

Creed grieved his fiancée. Months turned to years, the pain of murdering her by his own blade engulfing him, filling his days with darkness, and his nights with regrets. He obsessed over her ring for hours on end until eventually he stopped feeling anything at all. Over time he became hooked on the same narcotics that killed his family, in an effort to remember what feeling something was like.

But in a dark corner of his heart, something he'd tried to bury brewed. He had known all along how to feel again. Years and years passed before he decided to act. Creed could no longer deny the ecstasy he had felt when the last knife had fastened itself into Yasmin's heart.

It was a twisted, disturbing reality: taking her life, freeing her from this *sick* world. He realized that it was a freedom all men sought at the end — even though Yasmin's had come when least expected. He'd love to play a part in the process for others. It had dawned on him that to live was to know pain.

Finally, I've got another chance. To free mankind from its induced slavery.

A new man was reborn that moment. A man rising out of the ashes like a phoenix. As he stared at the new blades he'd purchased off the black market, a new resolve enveloped him. Along with a new name.

The Slayer.

WHO IS THE MAN BEHIND THE HOOD?

The news of the double homicide suspect's 'special delivery' to the police spread like wildfire, despite attempts to keep it under wraps. The media raged with the news for a long time, as speculations and counter-speculations flew around about the mysterious citizen who turned the culprit into the police. Here and there, one major question was raised. Was Mazono getting another vigilante?

In the meantime, enough evidence was gathered to nail the copycat for the double homicide, and he was jailed. After he was imprisoned, and after the media frenzy surrounding the way he was apprehended died down, everybody went about their normal business. Detective Roenega found himself dreading the thought of yet another wannabe vigilante running around. His father had told him stories of the Judge, and how much more difficult his job had been because of him.

He hoped things would soon return to normal, but they didn't. Drug peddlers started showing up bound and gagged in front of the station. Women started telling stories of a hooded individual who saved them from getting mugged. An increasing number of thieves got caught right as they broke in. It was almost as if the vigilante purposely waited for them to commit the crime before swooping in and catching them red-handed. In the case of the muggers, they were soundly beaten to within an inch of their lives.

As time went on, the description of the mysterious savior became more exaggerated with each narrative. Some people swore that he could fly; that he was the Superman of Mazono, and it was about time they had a superhero anyway.

A young lady insisted that he had superhuman strength and could lift objects ten times bigger than he was. This particular lady's statement was, however, negated by the fact she had been under the influence of a date rape drug when the mysterious figure had shown up just in time to save her from her would-be assailants. Still, she insisted that he had saved her life by breaking down the metal door to the room where a group of leering young men had been about to have their way with her, and then he beat them to a pulp.

A young man told the press about how he had been saved by a mysterious man wearing a crimson hoodie just as a group of gangsters had been about to 'teach him a lesson' for daring to stand up to one of their own.

Reports started coming in about sightings of the mysterious man on the roofs of various houses. The media had a field day with the news: newspapers ran the story of Mazono's mysterious law enforcer on their front pages. Both the fantastic and realistic descriptions of the mysterious individual were published in the newspapers and gossip tabloids.

However, in the midst of the various contradicting and sometimes downright ridiculous descriptions of the figure, a picture started to emerge. This man, whoever he was, wore a crimson hoodie with a mask almost completely obscuring his face. His voice, when he spoke, sounded rather deep and rumbling, but had a strange timbre, as if the man were struggling to speak.

This was a man that planned to remain incognito at all costs. However, his distinguishing feature, the one point on which everybody agreed, was his choice of weapon. The man carried a quiver of arrows, which he secured to his back with shoulder straps. If any of the witnesses were to be believed, the man had incredibly accurate aim. As one victim hastily claimed, the man could probably hit a target halfway around the world with his bow and arrow.

Newspapers started referring to him as the 'Crimson Arrow' based on his attire and his chosen weapon. Letters written to various newspapers either praised or denigrated the new vigilante of the city. While a section of the people felt that he should be given a medal, another section was of the opinion that he should stop. However, these different factions had one similar question in mind, as they were wont to ask. *Who was the man behind the hood?*

Looking perplexed, Johnny threw a newspaper on the table. As he did so, Barney walked in carrying a briefcase.

"Why the confused look?" Barney asked as he put the briefcase on one of the tables. The basement had changed since their operation hit full-swing. Purchasing one new device after another, the basement looked like the headquarters of a spy operation.

Johnny walked to the huge screen taking up one wall, the master computer that allowed Barney to get the feed from all the security cameras in the city.

"It really amazes me how you did all this," Johnny said. It had taken Barney some time, but he'd finally figured out how to hack the city's system.

"Glad you're finally appreciating my brilliance, Johnny Boy," Barney retorted, gesturing to the myriad of small boxes on the screen, each showing a different part of the city. "With this set-up, I can see almost all of Mazono from right here. My tech skills and your funding are a match made in heaven."

"This can direct me to crime scenes as soon as we see the signs of trouble," Johnny agreed.

"You've got it," Barney said.

"They're calling me the Crimson Arrow now, by the way," Johnny said, amused. "For crying out loud, I think I preferred the Cleaner." Then he noticed the way Barney was looking at him. "You look awfully proud of yourself there, Barn."

Barney simply grinned, looking like an alcoholic that had just been led to a fountain of ever-flowing beer. "Maybe you should check out what's in the briefcase first."

Johnny shot him a questioning look, then headed for the table on which the briefcase sat, talking the whole time. "This should be interesting," he said as he opened it. On seeing the contents of the briefcase, he trailed off, awed.

"Well," Barney sounded positively smug. "I hope it's to your liking."

Johnny reached into the briefcase and drew out what looked at first glance like a hooded jumpsuit. The fabric was supple and somewhat stretchy, promising ease of mobility to the wearer. A logo that looked like a bow at first glance, but was actually the capital letter "A" tucked sideways into the letter "C," was emblazoned on the front of the suit.

"Oh wow," Johnny said.

"I know, right?" Barney replied. "It also comes with a microphone and auditory device in the event that you ever have to plant a bug anywhere. There's a two-way communication system installed that allows me to see and hear everything you do."

"This... this is...I wasn't expecting..."

"Well, if you're going to be cleaning up the streets, you ought to do it in style, yeah? Why don't you try it on?" Barney was beaming from ear to ear.

Johnny had already started tugging his clothes off. "This is amazing!" he exclaimed as he pulled the suit on.

"Hmm…" Barney replied thoughtfully as he walked around his friend, assessing the fit of the suit and the functionality of certain features. "How's the hood?"

"Much better than the last one," Johnny replied as Barney showed him how to turn on the communication system. "This is great, Barney. I feel like a superhero. Like the Judge."

"Hmmm," Barney replied, preoccupied with double-checking his computer to ensure that he was connected to Johnny's suit. When he finally satisfied himself, he turned around to face his friend and held out his hand. In his hand was a bracelet.

"You'll need this as well. It's a tracker. Hit that small button and it'll immediately signal me. It took me time to get the functions working in conjunction with each other, you know. I just kept thinking I'd missed something, but couldn't place a finger on it."

"Yeah, I remember; you told me about it. How did you fix the glitch?"

Barney recalled the memory thoughtfully. "Well, I was working on the schematics during my free time at work, and one of the senior executives who happened to be around at that time had been watching me for awhile. You must have seen him around - receding hairline, has a dark stubble on his chin-"

"The guy you said hasn't shaved in like two years? Doctor…Wang. Right?"

"That's kind of blunt but yes, that's the guy. Eventually, he walked up to me, pointed out the flaw like it was nothing, and walked away. After he mentioned it, the problem seemed so obvious that I felt embarrassed at having missed it all this time." Barney shook his head. "Stupid. Just stupid. All I needed to do was to-"

"No, no, Barney, please keep speaking English," Johnny replied, afraid he was about to launch into yet another of his complicated lectures about binary or operating systems. "You know I don't understand you when you go into Barney mode."

Barney shook his head and concluded his narration. "Anyway, after I fixed it, all the systems started working like a charm. It was ridiculous how simple it was, really."

Johnny frowned as a thought came to him. "But wouldn't Wang have wondered what you were designing the system for?"

Barney shrugged. "I don't think it would have mattered to him. I'm almost always tinkering with something in my free time, trying to figure out how something can be made more efficient, faster, and better. He's far too self-centered to have taken notice of what I was really doing. He's in the tech industry and refers to himself as a doctor for crying out loud. Wang is legendary around the office for his inability to remember even most of our names. I don't think we'll have any problems."

Johnny looked at the suit once more. "Crimson Arrow, huh."

"I guess we're really in business now."

Barney stood up and fist-bumped his friend.

"Dispatch to all units." The police radio crackled to life, halting Barney and Johnny as they sparred. "There's been a grand larceny at the Mazono City Bank. Suspect's getaway car is a gray truck. The Chief wants him caught. By any means necessary."

"What do we have here?" Barney said, facing Johnny and wiping his brow with a hand towel. "Are you thinking what I'm thinking?"

"I know what you're thinking," Johnny said, walking to the fridge to grab a bottle of water. "Though, I'd strongly advise that we leave this one to the cops. This isn't really my area of expertise. Besides, how will this help us find April's killer?"

"Since when did we start to believe in the cops' ability to get shit done? It's the right thing to do. She would want you to help."

"I knew you were gonna say that," Johnny sighed, after draining half the bottle's contents.

"Well? Get to it," Barney said, gesturing towards the motorcycle on the far side of the lair.

"You don't need to ask."

"I didn't."

"Just tell me where I need to go."

Barney sighed and began searching the screens furiously for the vehicle in question. Soon, a dot appeared on the screen. It was blinking as it moved from one point to the next. "Gotcha!"

"Where's the van?" Johnny's voice sounded distant, as he backed away from Barney, opening a drawer containing his vigilante suit.

"Fifth Avenue. That's only a couple of blocks away from where we are right now."

"Sucks for them," Johnny said, easing into his suit. He grabbed his quiver filled with arrows and slung it over his shoulder. Finally, he threw the hood over his head. "How's it look?"

"Like an eighth-grader who's gone to Prom thinking it's Halloween."

"Asshole." Johnny rolled his eyes.

Barney laughed. "Don't forget to turn on your coms."

The suspect floored the pedal of the nondescript truck past another red traffic light. It grumbled, bursting forward, cutting through another intersection, the sirens from the cop cars fading in the distance. He smiled.

The heist had been smooth. The operation was discreet. No one was supposed to know what was going down.

No loopholes. No leads for the cops. No trail.

The robber raced through the night, his truck loaded with duffel bags filled with cash. He could think of a hundred ways to spend the cash, and still be set for life.

With my cut, I'll fly under the radar for about six months. Then I'll travel out West and set up a mini casino, or a clubhouse, after making sure to clean the cash, of course. Or marry a fine-ass lady and spend the next summer overseas for the honeymoon, or travel South, and —

An arrow sliced through the truck's back window and lodged in the dashboard. The driver swerved the vehicle, momentarily stunned. A duffel bag had fallen on the road by the time he regained control. He cussed under his breath, staring wistfully through the rear-view mirror as the breeze began to splay the bag's contents.

He had heard rumors of a vigilante prowling the streets, bringing criminals to justice, his signature weapon an arrow. He never believed such fables. *Those are stories you tell to kids to make them believe that there's some good left in the world.* Now, as he raced through another red light, evading the cops, he wondered if he had been wrong all along. He floored the pedal harder this time.

He was already turning left at the next intersection when a sharp hissing sound emanated behind him, then the scratching sound of metal scraping pavement hit his ears. The truck swerved and smashed off the pole of a street light, then continued racing forward, its speed slowed. He realized with horror that an arrow was sticking out of the rear tire of the truck.

Who the hell is this guy?!?

The cops were closing in on him. If his truck continued running like this, the cops would be on him in no time.

He was on the brink of hitting the brakes when another arrow struck the second rear tire. The force of the shot, coupled with the brake, forced him to swerve again, this time toppling the truck. Duffel bags splayed all over the road, as the truck's windows shattered to smithereens. His head had slammed against the steering wheel when the truck began toppling, and his nostrils oozed crimson. From the corner of his eye, he saw the police cars were close, the sirens screaming louder with each passing second.

Before he knew it, cops surrounded his truck.

"Get out of the car, and put your hands in the air!" a megaphone crackled, the voice behind it sounding excited.

"I can't," he yelled from inside the vehicle, howling in pain. "I'm stuck. Fuck, I'm stuck!"

The cops cornered him and pulled him out of the truck.

"You're under arrest, whoever you are, and you –"

His hands were already up. He was going to come in quietly. Being impaled by an arrow was definitely not on his to-do list. As long as he didn't talk, the boss wouldn't care.

From atop a penthouse, a couple of blocks from the arrest scene, the Crimson Arrow stood, watching the transpiring scene.

"You did it, Johnny," the voice of Barney Smith whispered in his ear.

"You're wrong, Barn," Johnny said, watching as the bank-robbing murderer was deposited into the backseat of a police car. Handcuffed. "We did it."

"I hate it when you call me Barn."

Johnny said nothing, retreating back into the shadows.

Another criminal down. The sky was looking beautiful tonight.

Detective Dusty Roenega cursed. This Crimson Arrow business was getting out of hand. What was he going to do about it? Not only had the blasted man made the police look like incompetent fools; now Dusty had to deal with the press. Far more contact with them than he liked.

As far as Roenega was concerned, the press was nothing but a school of sharks, hungrily seeking smaller fish to fill their bloodlust. Right now, he felt like one of those smaller fish, and he thoroughly resented that feeling. The department had been bombarded with calls and messages from reporters wanting to take a statement from the police, wanting information, wanting something they could publish in newspapers, air on the radio, broadcast on television. Roenega did not like this sudden interest in the police department.

Detective Roenega marshalled his thoughts to focus on the woman sitting opposite him. She had introduced herself as Ashley Hayes, a reporter with the Mazono Press, one of the more prestigious newspapers in the city. He had done his best to avoid this meeting, hoping she would deal with whatever vague statement she got from the PR people and the Chief of Police, but she was dogged in her insistence to set up an interview with him. Finally, he had succumbed to her request simply to be rid of her. With an effort, he flashed what he hoped was a pleasant smile.

"Detective, what do you have to say about the activities of this so-called Crimson Arrow who's running amok in the city? Have any efforts been made to subdue the vigilante behind the hood?"

Roenega sighed inwardly. This reporter was obviously not in the vigilante's camp.

"Naturally, I cannot disclose much at this time. But I assure you that efforts are being made to find this Crimson Arrow, whoever he is, and curb his activities. The last thing we need is for citizens of Mazono to think that they can take the law into their own hands."

Ashley stared at him, clearly underwhelmed with his response. After a few seconds, she jotted down some notes.

"What about the reports flying around that the Crimson Arrow is working with the police? According to reliable sources, the man brings criminals to the station, tied and gagged."

"And more often than not, beaten within an inch of their lives," Roenega shot back. "When we take the bad guys down, we try to use minimal force. We don't just beat them up at will. Seems to me like this vigilante carries out his own judgment on the criminals, then brings them here simply to give the appearance of being on the side of justice. This man, whoever he is, is obviously violent and insensitive, irrational even, probably somebody with a vendetta of sorts. The last thing we need right now is someone carrying out his own personal crusade in this city."

Ashley nodded. "One last question, Detective."

Perfect. He thought.

"What will be done to this Crimson Arrow character when he is eventually apprehended?"

Tread softly, Dusty.

"Ah…that question really is not one I can answer. But I am absolutely confident that at the end of the day, justice will be served."

She appeared disappointed with his generic answer. She leaned forward, turned off her tape recorder, and then started to pack her things into a large handbag. "Thank you for your time, Detective."

"You're welcome." *Don't come back.*

As Ashley walked out of the building, her mind swirled with ideas. She needed to get this interview ready for the midweek edition of the newspaper. She smiled to herself, proud that she had finally been able to corner Detective Roenega and irk him enough to get his opinion on at least one of her questions. Still, his non-answers to her other questions annoyed her, though she was used to it.

Ever since the news of the Crimson Arrow hit the media, she had been against the idea of a lone vigilante taking on the criminal underworld in Mazono City. There were those who made him out to be a cross between a superhero and a demi-god, but she was not one of them. She knew better. Ashley Hayes believed in due procedure, and that the saga of this menace running around the city with a bow and arrow could only end in disaster.

The smell of sweat hung briefly in the air of the halogen-lit basement. Johnny was striking and ducking rhythmically at a punching bag dangling from the concrete slab above him. His bones ached as he rammed a right hook into the bag. He looked beyond the bag, distracted by and admiring the new set of bows propped at the left end of the building.

His parents were all too delighted to bequeath their possessions to him when he came home on the weekend and innocently requested their old training equipment. They didn't bother to ask him the object of this new fascination; they knew that with the loss of April, Johnny would benefit from a new pastime. They were all too eager to assist him.

Barney, on the other hand, was lying down on a bench and lifting 100lb dumbbells, the muscles on his exposed arms tightening and spreading around his chest as the motion intensified.

...16. 17. 18. 19. 20.

The main computer suddenly began to beep, making Barney pause mid-air. He carefully placed each weight on the floor.

"You couldn't have picked a less annoying alarm?" Johnny asked, ducking as the bag swept past his head, and landing another right hook on it as it came into focus.

Barney shook his head, grabbing a towel and wiping his face. Heaving a sigh of relief, he grabbed a bottle of water from the fridge, briefly stealing a glance at the monitor's screen. What he saw made him pause, the surprise registering on his face.

"Johnny," he said, rushing to sit in his chair facing the monitor. "Come, see this."

Johnny steadied the bag as it swung towards him, grabbed another towel, and walked to the pulsing screen.

"This feed was pulled up from a street camera five minutes ago," Barney said, filling the screen with video feed from a street camera.

In the footage, a white van with the Mazono General Hospital logo emblazoned on the side halted at an intersection, one that Johnny didn't recognize, waiting for the red lights to switch to green. It was difficult to spot the driver behind the wheel, but he could make out the outlines of his hands grasped on the steering wheel.

Suddenly, a Mazono Elite Sedan screeched to a halt in front of the van. The doors swung open, and two men leapt out of the car. Before the driver of the van could react, one of the men raised a gun. A flash of light — no sound — and the next second, a bullet hole appeared in the van's windshield.

The footage was black-and-white, and a dark shade appeared on the windshield. Johnny suddenly registered it as crimson. The color drained from Johnny's face. One man from the car approached the van, opened the door and dragged out the driver, dropping him to the pavement. When the driver clutched his arm with his other hand, Johnny let out a sigh, relieved that the man was still alive.

The man who'd shot the driver of the van walked briskly to the car he'd arrived in and jetted off. The other man from the car got into the van and drove after him.

Slowly, the van driver crawled across the road, his face contorted in agony. He pulled himself to his feet, leaning against a streetlight pole.

"Barney, call an ambulance," Johnny said as he grabbed his costume, "and tell me where those bastards are headed."

"On it."

The next second, Barney was speaking to a 911 agent. "One man badly wounded, at the intersection between Fourth and Mason. Needs an ambulance. ASAP!" He severed the connection before the agent asked for his details, or before the line could be traced.

"Where to?" Johnny asked, zipping up his costume, his face cold.

"Hold on," Barney replied, keying a series of commands into the screen. "Got it. They just pulled up into a warehouse close to the seaport. I'm pulling up the schematics of the place."

Johnny walked towards the glass panel containing all the weapons he'd collected from his parents, and some he'd discreetly purchased off a black market using a front. He ran his fingers over each weapon before picking up the usual: a black bow and a set of arrows arranged in a quiver with a magnetic strap. Deliberating briefly, he grabbed a variety of grenades as well.

"Johnny," Barney called. "I'm picking up multiple vehicles inside the warehouse from past footage. Be careful."

Johnny nodded.

"Last thing," Barney added. "Assume they're all armed."

"Of course they are," Johnny growled. "I'm taking the bike."

A short whistling sound pierced the air as the warehouse garage door descended, the van and Elite safely in its confines. The sea's waves lapped against the dock as the night breeze blew. Apart from a yacht setting sail in the distance, there was no one in sight. The two security detail on night shift who were supposed to man the lighthouse had taken the night off. The police seldom patrolled this location. The place was as quiet as an empty hall.

Inside the soundproof walls, a machine rattled idly. The warehouse housed a lab at the far end where several men, dressed in white laboratory coats, safety goggles, and gloves, barked orders to others in casual clothes who rushed off to do their bidding. Sophisticated equipment lay on working tables. A green liquid brewed effervescent inside a cylindrical container over a

Bunsen burner. A white powdered substance—cocaine—was being mixed in batches and stored in cartons.

Above the ramp, Ryder, a man in his late forties, looked on, glass in hand, as the activities progressed.

The doors of the Elite and the van opened, and the two men who'd shot the van driver slid out.

"Boss," one of the men called out, walking towards Ryder. "We found the van occupying that intersection just like you said it would."

"Makes me wonder how you got your inside man," the other said.

"That's the kind of statement that gets you killed, mangled beyond recognition, and dumped in parts of the sea where the sharks feed."

"Uhh…my bad," the man said as a chill raced up his spine.

Ryder, a conduit for one of the bigwigs in Mazono, snapped his fingers, and men rushed to the back of the van. He smiled. His boss would be pleased with his efforts.

Their inside man, who worked in the General Hospital, gave them the schedule of the vans carrying supplies, on the condition that none of the drivers be killed. The shot to the driver's arm earlier had been a targeted hit. Nothing a few days at the hospital wouldn't fix.

As Ryder watched the men work, something skidded past the corner of his eyes. He blinked to be certain he wasn't hallucinating. He shot sharp glances around the facility. Nothing was out of place.

It must be the booze, he thought.

He wanted to wrap things up quickly and call it a night. But work was far from finished, with the next day's batch yet to be prepared.

A blood-curdling scream broke the silence as Ryder turned to enter his makeshift office. He stopped in his tracks, his hands moving to grab the pistol from his holster. As if on cue, everyone else — including the cronies in lab coats — grabbed their weapons, raising and aiming them toward the sound.

"Who's that?"

As if timed down to the second, the metal doors of the warehouse exploded. The vibration threw everything within a ten-foot radius farther into the building. Before the chaos dissipated, a man — unseen — slid into the building.

Silence lingered in the warehouse, save for the machine still whirring idly in the lab.

What happened next was fast, even for Ryder's mind to process. An arrow shot from the inky darkness where the scream had emanated, and smashed one of the halogen lights, throwing the room into partial darkness. Another followed shortly, sinking into the arms of one of the henchmen.

"The Crimson Arrow," Ryder cried, circling backward towards his office. "Kill him!" he screamed.

Johnny ducked and rolled across the warehouse floor to where utility equipment was stored, as a hail of bullets followed him. Ryder rushed into his office as the gunfire raged below.

On Ryder's table were pages containing confidential documents, clients' addresses, and a payroll. Ryder knew that if the vigilante laid his fingers on any of this, the police would have a field day, tracking every single member of their group and making them testify in court.

One of the workers was bound to reveal who they really worked for. The boss would kill him for that.

I can't let that happen.

He grabbed everything on the worktable, crumpled it all together and hurled it into a metal bin. Then he lit a lighter and threw it into the bin.

Satisfied that the fire was enveloping everything in the pile, he walked to the corner of the room where a cupboard stood. The gunshots were getting thinner with every passing second. Pushing the cupboard aside, he entered a four-digit code into an electronic lock, and a wall whistled.

It was a door.

Ryder had never used this secret door before. He'd never needed to. Through it, he now slid out of the office, clicked the door shut, and ran towards the dock where his ride sat. The gunshots petered as Ryder started the vehicle and drove off.

Back in the warehouse, Johnny contemplated his options: from his calculations, there were four men left. The rest were either howling on the ground with an arrow sticking out of them, or knocked out cold. The resolve to finish them consumed him, but he resisted. Any wrong move he made could cost him his life.

He scanned the floor again. The men were approaching dangerously close. Aiming for the overhead lights, he let an arrow fly. It crashed into the light, shattering the glass, and producing the blinding effect he was after.

The men stumbled as they dodged away from the falling shards. Johnny swung to the opposite side, another arrow swirling from his bow into the hip of one of the men, its momentum flinging him backward.

Johnny crept quietly, ears alert for movement. Another man ran past, and Johnny spun in an arc, sweeping him off his feet. Before the man could react, Johnny delivered him a crushing blow. He blacked out.

Two left.

As he slunk towards the corner, he noticed the two men were not in sight. He activated his communication system with Barney. A sharp movement to his right caught his attention. Soon he heard the crunching of steps on his left.

They're trying to corner me.

Moving quietly, he grabbed a piece of steel from the utility table and tossed it a couple of feet. The result was as expected: the metal made a loud clanking on the concrete floor. Immediately, a torrent of bullets peppered the metal. The sparks of light from the gun barrels as the bullets exited them revealed the men's locations.

Johnny ran to the left, throwing a right hook into one brute, then twirled and shot another blow into his jaw. The man yelped in pain as he crashed face-first onto the ground.

The last man tried to reload his weapon as he watched Johnny take down his comrade, but before the bullet could be clipped in place, Johnny was on him. A shock of recognition flashed across Johnny's face as he stared at the man.

It was the man who had shot the van driver.

In a flash, Johnny pinned him to the ground, grabbed the lapel of his shirt and began choking him out.

"Finish him, Johnny."

"Not now," he growled back.

"He's a criminal. He deserves it."

He loosened his grip as the man's body faded, out cold.

He walked slowly to the entrance and looked around. "Don't do that again, Barney. Ever. Now, what's the status of the driver?"

"A rescue team with an ambulance arrived at the scene and took him away."

"Alert the police. I'm done here."

"I've been tracking 911 calls routed within a mile radius of that vicinity. Two calls were made about seven minutes ago. You would know if you'd switched on your coms earlier." Johnny noticed the tone of apprehension on Barney's voice.

"Yeah, but then I would have to listen to your kill-the-bad-guy bullshit. I'd rather take my chances at getting shot."

"Johnny."

"Yeah, I know. Sorry."

"Wait, I didn't get that."

"Yes, you did."

Chuckles.

"Johnny, the police are on their way, taking the main route. If I were you, I'd stay out of their way. Take the street path, it's barely ever used, but it'll get you here in…" Johnny heard a couple of commands pressed. "…in about twenty minutes, give or take."

"I'll see you soon," Johnny said, severing the connection and getting on his bike. As he raced through the street path, he heard the sounds of sirens rending the night air.

"Boss," Ryder panted as he walked into the office of his employer. "The Crimson Arrow struck the warehouse. Thankfully, I escaped."

The room was dark save for the light pooling from the window, the skyline of Mazono visible through the glass. The man backed away from the window, a cigar in his hand. He sighed as he settled into his chair. It was hard to read his face, causing Ryder to jitter unsteadily on his feet.

"Ryder, tell me everything that happened," the man said, taking a long drag.

Ryder recounted everything, from the pickup of the van, till he'd run into the office and burnt everything that would tie his employer to the narcotics.

The boss nodded when Ryder was done. "That was a wise thing to do, burning those documents before the cops or the Crimson Arrow laid their hands on them."

Ryder beamed. His boss was pleased with his actions. "Yes, boss. And the workers don't know who I report to, so nothing will be linked back to you."

"That's where you're wrong," the man said, raising his left hand. Firmly clasped in it was a .9mm caliber silencer pistol. "You will be linked back to me."

Ryder didn't hear the sound of the bullet, nor did he take notice when it slammed into his forehead.

He only realized that his body was falling, and sensed the darkness engulfing him as he thudded to the ground.

The man pressed a button on his desk. "Send in the cleaners. They've got work to do tonight."

A lone house stood on a hill on the outskirts of Mazono. Rays of sun filtered through the wooden fence surrounding the perimeter, casting a dull glow on the grounds. A little farmhouse, it was inhabited by a hermit who chose its secluded location to keep the world out.

Normally, the place looked like any regular farmhouse. Today though, the house was surrounded by parked cars and muscular men wearing suits and dark glasses, their bodies tense and alert. It looked like something big was going down there.

The inside of the house was normal. The furnishings and décor were sparse, which could be attributed to the eccentricity of the hermit who lived there. Usually occupied only by the hermit and his farmhands, today the house was overrun by men who appeared grim and alert. They all got to their feet as a tall, well-dressed man entered.

Eric Marcoso, a respected businessman well-known for his ever-growing financial empire as well as his philanthropy, appeared to the public as the embodiment of a generous, kind-hearted businessman. Had they known, however, that he led the largest smuggling ring in the city, or how he killed men without blinking as he had murdered Ryder last night, they would probably hold a different opinion.

As it was, Marcoso worked hard to ensure that his shadier business interests stayed well hidden. As he strode into the room, he noticed he was the last to arrive. Four men and a woman were already gathered around the conference table. Marcoso stepped in, and the door closed.

The atmosphere in the room was tense. Gathered were the movers and shakers of Mazono, influential individuals who called the shots in the city. They were here for one reason. They did not take kindly to anything or anyone that posed a threat to their continued influence in society. And today, they felt threatened.

Marcoso sat at the head of the table, his piercing eyes taking in the grave look on each face. He could see that these people would do anything to eliminate the threat they felt.

"I apologize for my tardiness, gentlemen … Donna," he said cordially. "I hope I haven't kept you waiting long."

They mumbled their replies.

Eric Taylor spoke up. "Well, at least you're here now, so let's get this meeting started. I have goods to ship, both above and below the table, and I'd like to get back to it."

Marcoso nodded, hiding his annoyance at Taylor's tone. "Indeed. Without wasting any time, I'll get right to the heart of the matter. We have a serious problem facing us; one that will prove fatally damaging to our respective interests if nothing is done to stop it."

All around the room, there were nods of agreement.

Leaning forward, Marcoso picked up the file in front of him. Identical files sat on the table in front of each person in the room, and they all reached for theirs simultaneously.

A detailed report on the Crimson Arrow sat before them. Reference was made to articles, eyewitness accounts, everything known to pertain to the activities of the vigilante. Although he'd already read the file cover to cover,

Marcoso now skimmed through it again to reacquaint himself with its contents. Finally, he sighed heavily and put the file down.

"I'm sure you will all agree with me that this…this vigilante, known as the Crimson Arrow, is fast becoming a hindrance to our activities," he began. Several heads nodded in agreement. "This report in front of us tells us everything except what we really need to know: who is this man? What makes him think he can just meddle in our business like this?"

"He's probably a lunatic with a messiah complex, we see it all the time in court," said Dean Fletcher, an influential judge who had swayed many a sentencing in favor of the people in this room.

"Well, there is a method to his madness, if that be the case," growled Phillip Johnson. "Not far back, this Arrow person intercepted a man of mine leaving the bank. I don't know how he did it, but the tires of the vehicle my man left in were punctured by arrows. Now my guy's in custody. Thankfully he'd never talk."

Johnson leaned forward in his chair, visibly agitated. "This isn't the first time the bastard has meddled in my business, and it's beginning to wear on me. I only ran that last gig because he'd thwarted a few others. Every time he attacks, I lose merchandise worth hundreds of thousands of dollars. I'm losing money, and to be blunt, I'm absolutely sick of it." He leaned back in his chair.

"I've also encountered this menace in my business transactions," said Donna Henshaw bitterly. "I can barely afford to meet my clients' needs anymore, and that's because my supply link has been severed by this lunatic, and I think my clients are beginning to look elsewhere for their supplies. You don't just replace A-Listers as clients. This vigilante, self-proclaimed hero, whatever he is, needs to be stopped."

"What I'd like to know is how he knows what's going on all over the city at seemingly every hour," blurted Taylor. "He's making it harder and harder for me to stock my stores and I'm losing money," he spat angrily.

"Something must be done about this man," Doug Thompson said, quietly. Doug Thompson, the oldest and most respected member at the table, was a quiet, brooding man whose large stature inspired awe and fear. Dressed like a cultured gentleman, everyone present knew his prowess in combat. He was a man to be feared, and nobody liked to cross him, not even Marcoso. All eyes turned to him, and he looked at Marcoso. "You know what we have to do," he said simply.

Marcoso held his gaze for a while, then nodded. "Indeed. I'm sure you all agree that Crimson Arrow needs to be dealt with as soon as possible." He didn't wait for a reply before continuing. "It is a moot point to state that his activities have proven detrimental to us in many ways."

"Get to the point, Marcoso," said Johnson.

Once more, Marcoso kept his irritation in check as he spoke. "I propose we get rid of this thug as soon, and as efficiently, as possible. We need to send a message. This is our town, and we will not let anybody take it away from us."

Fletcher looked doubtful. "I'm in complete agreement with you, but how do you propose we do this?"

"I was just getting to that, Dean," Marcoso replied. Then he sat back and looked thoughtfully at Thompson. "Doug, we both know this is more your field than mine. Why don't you take the floor?"

Doug nodded, reached into his briefcase, and brought out some files, which he passed across to the other occupants of the room.

"Like Dean has pointed out," Doug Thompson said, "we need more than our usual petty criminals to take out this…unwanted element. Now, over my illustrious career in this business, I've been able to meet and make the acquaintance of certain unique individuals, some of whom have very special talents that set them apart from your everyday hire. They don't come cheap, but they will definitely give you value for your money."

He opened the file. "I'll start with Deadeye. He's the premier marksman in the world. He's an astonishingly accurate sniper with a first shot success rate of over ninety-seven percent. The Crimson Arrow might be good with his antiquated weapons, but I assure you that if he were ever to come across Deadeye, he would be ended before he could even draw his bow."

He turned to the next page. It was an image of a foreign-looking man with long dark hair, wearing a smirk nearly as big as his trench coat. "Victor Sheath. He's an expert, no, a genius, with explosives. If you need someone to blow someone or something up, Sheath is your man. He's a bit of a showman, which in turn is the result of his love for the dramatic and sensational. But he knows how to get things done."

Then he turned the next page. "Alana Fitzpatrick. She's the quintessential femme fatale. She's beautiful, seductive, and deadly. Lethal in hand-to-hand combat, and adept at making you believe whatever she wants you to believe." He chuckled. "She has the face of an angel and the cunning of a snake, and she will do whatever it takes to get her quarry. I've made her acquaintance a number of times. She is not someone I will soon forget."

He turned yet another page. "I think you all will appreciate this one. The Omega Archer."

"Another bow-and-arrow nutcase?" scoffed Johnson.

Doug shot him a dark look. "The Omega Archer is anything *but* a nutcase. In fact, his mind is clearer and sharper than anybody's in this room. Yes, he is also quite adept at using the bow and arrow, but beyond that, he is a man of immense pride, one who does not only get the job done but ensures that it is done well."

"Lastly, we have Scooter. While I'm sure you find this unusual name amusing, I assure you that Zach Moreno, as he was born, does not. It's a childhood nickname that he cherishes. However, you care not for what he is named, but for *what he can do*. He is a physical marvel, a literal superhuman with super strength, super reflexes, accelerated healing, and elite hand-to-hand combat skills. I'd love to meet whoever engineered such a being. Only Omega is as feared in the underworld. Now, Scooter does go by a code where he will not kill. However, he is more than willing to hand-deliver the product to the buyer."

He finally put the file down and looked at the others in the room. "These are no ordinary henchmen. In fact, each one would kill you just for referring to them with that word. They are world-class assassins. Each of them is lethal, brilliant, and resourceful. We'll need all of that and more if we are going to eliminate this Crimson Arrow."

"But how do we get them to come here?" Fletcher asked.

"That's easy," Doug replied. "Rather than contact each of them individually, I have a plan that will get all of them here with one goal in mind: to get rid of the Crimson Arrow." Then he stopped and let the tension in the room build. "But I'll need your help."

Taylor leaned forward, intrigued. "How?"

"These people are all trained assassins. Killing is their skill. And like all skilled workers, a certain…incentive…is required to pique their interest." He stopped and saw the light of understanding dawn in the eyes of his audience. "It will be the magnet that will bring them here in the first place. But, like I've said, these are no ordinary assassins. Our offer must be worth their time."

"So, what exactly are you suggesting?" Phillip Johnson asked.

Doug shot him another dark look. The man really was getting on his nerves. "I propose, with the approval of everyone here, that we place a bounty on the Crimson Arrow. Five million dollars dead, ten million alive, so we can teach him a lesson."

"A bounty?" asked Donna. "But wouldn't that bring other assassins here too?"

"Yes, it will," replied Doug, "but regard that as an added advantage. Any lesser assassins may or may not be able to stop the Crimson Arrow, but they can slow him down, weaken him, distract him, and make the job even easier for our more accomplished guests."

"And Mazono will be overrun by assassins and the crime rates will skyrocket," Fletcher muttered.

"That's the short-term," Doug said. "We have become who we are today by thinking long-term. It's a small price to pay if we intend to sustain our hold on this city. Upon success, we'll make that money up in mere months. As it is, our power is consistently weakening, consistently hacked away by the activities of this vermin, whoever he is. The best way to deal with this problem is to annihilate it swiftly and cleanly, by any means possible. Are we in agreement or not?"

Each person in the room looked at Eric Marcoso, who was flipping through the pages in front of him. Finally, he began to say something, but Philip Johnson cut in.

"There is one other avenue we could explore," Johnson said. Both Marcoso and Thompson looked at him, instantly wary. There was something smug about the way Philip sounded. Sending a triumphant look at Doug, he reached into his briefcase and brought out a file. Doug caught a glimpse of what was written on the front and instantly shot to his feet, his eyes narrowed.

"Put that away, Phil," he said, his voice ominously low.

Johnson looked at him, his eyes filled with defiance. "Why should I?" he spat. "We are looking for a way to get rid of our mutual problem, aren't we? We should explore all avenues."

Doug cautioned him, his face full of warning and menace. "Phil, we will have nothing to do with that…monster." The other people in the room, Marcoso excluded, looked on, bewildered at what was happening. Marcoso simply sat back and folded his arms, his gaze levelled on Phil, eyes hard as stone.

"Listen to the man, Phil," Marcoso said.

"But I insist…"

"We will have nothing to do with him!" Doug roared. The others looked on, nervous. They had never heard Doug raise his voice before.

"Oh, so now you're afraid," Phil taunted. "Do you know how much money I've lost this month? Maybe you shou—"

The sound of a gunshot ricocheted in the room, drowning out the rest of his words. As the others looked on, horrified, Phil slid off the chair and thudded to the floor, blood flowing from a bullet hole in his head. Doug grimly pocketed his gun and picked up the file. On the cover was a single word.

Goode.

As quickly as possible, Doug tucked the file inside the dead man's briefcase and zipped it shut. Then he settled into his chair calmly, grabbed the glass of vodka in front of him, raised it to the air, and took a swig of the drink amidst the stunned gazes trained at him.

He let out a sigh. *Thank God. He would have ruined everything.*

WAS THAT REALLY NECESSARY?

The ensuing silence following the gunshot was deafening in its intensity. For a long time, the others in the room, excluding Marcoso, could only look, horrified, at the body on the floor being enveloped in a slowly spreading pool of blood.

Marcoso finally broke the silence. "I'm sorry about that," he said mildly, sounding for all the world as if he was talking about a child that had just thrown a slightly embarrassing tantrum. "But you will all have to take my word for it when I say that he was getting ahead of himself." The others only looked on, dumbfounded. Doug angrily shoved the briefcase under the table, a huge scowl on his face, the wheels in his head turning. Just how had that idiot gotten such an insane idea?

Marcoso was still speaking. "Why don't I get rid of this unpleasantness, hmm?" he said. Calmly, he pushed a button on the intercom and requested clean-up. A few minutes later, the door slid open, and about a half dozen men came in, two of them bearing a stretcher while others carried cleaning instruments. The men with the stretcher placed Phil's body on it and carried him out, while the others proceeded to mop up the blood. The whole thing was very quick and expertly done; in a few minutes, the floor was back to its pristine condition. After the men left, Marcoso smiled benignly. "Shall we get back to business?"

Dean Fletcher had lit a cigarette and was now puffing on it in agitation. Donna Henshaw, who had initially turned white as a sheet, was regaining color in her face. Eric Taylor folded his arms, then realizing that it might be misconstrued as a threatening stance, unfolded them, his hands shaking. It wasn't the act itself that affected them all so profoundly: it was the suddenness with which it had been carried out. No one had been expecting that. They had all heard tales of Doug Thompson's ruthlessness. Now they had witnessed it first-hand, and were visibly shaken.

Fletcher was the first to find his voice. "Was that really necessary? Couldn't it have waited until a more opportune time? What is in that file?"

Marcoso sighed. "I apologize for this unfortunate occurrence, Dean. I know it places you in a most awkward position. But, like I said earlier, Phil was getting ahead of himself. What he was about to do would have certainly cost us control of the city for good. You are all better off not knowing what contents lie inside. And you know Phil: he always had to have his way. He didn't know what he was getting himself into."

Donna took in a deep, calming breath. "Couldn't he have been stopped any other way?" She stole a quick glance at Doug Thompson, who beamed weakly at her.

"Like I've already said, I'm sorry, but it had to be done. When you see the things I've seen in my illustrious career, you learn the difference between men and monsters. Now, let's get back to business; I have a meeting with the mayor in an hour. I'm sure that between all of us, we can easily raise ten million dollars. We'll spread the news of the bounty tonight." He looked at Thompson, whose mouth was set in a grim line. "Thompson will see to it that it gets to all the relevant quarters."

"And what happens after that?" Taylor asked.

"We wait," Marcoso said. "We'll have issued our invitation; I'm sure our guests will want to enjoy the feast." He looked at his watch. "On that note, we'll end this meeting. I will inform the mayor about our decision so that he's not entirely left out. I'm sure he would also be kind enough to contribute to our cause, especially now that we are a member short. Enjoy the rest of your day, lady and gentlemen."

As if on cue, the door slid open, and the others filed out, still subdued and shaken by what had happened. Doug Thompson stayed behind to talk to Marcoso.

"How did he get that file?" Marcoso asked. Now that the others had left, he showed no restraint. He was visibly shaken.

"I have no idea," Doug replied, his face grim. "But it will no longer be a problem. I'll make sure no contact was made."

"Good."

AGOG WITH EXCITEMENT

By nightfall, news had spread like wildfire about the bounty placed on the Crimson Arrow. At Charlie's, the air was charged with excitement. All across the bar, the various patrons were bent towards each other, muttering excitedly.

Down Hollow Alley, not far from Charlie's, a man shuffled along. His bedraggled clothes were worn and dirty, and his hair was untidy, standing in unseemly clumps on his head. In one hand, he held a knife. Dragging his feet as he walked, it appeared as though he couldn't summon the energy to raise one foot up after the other. As he walked, his eyes veered from left to right.

There was a part in Hollow Alley where gangsters were known to gather. Colorful graffiti on the wall marked their spot, and no one dared to pass whenever they were there. Even the police had an unspoken agreement to avoid the area. In fact, most people had given up on using Hollow Alley, preferring to find alternative and safer routes home. The bedraggled man, however, was above the rules of those beneath him. Those few who'd tangled with him and were still alive had scars that bore testament to his ruthlessness. A long while back, an uneasy truce had been established between the man and the gangs in the Backstreets: *stay out of my way, and I may stay out of yours.*

Today, the gangsters were gathered at their usual spot, all whispering amongst themselves. A small part of the ragged man wondered what all the excitement was about. He had noticed an undercurrent of…something in the air, but he had not cared enough to find out what it was.

He had survived thus far with the bare minimum of contact with other members of the human race, and he intended to keep things that way. He had more important things to worry about. Specifically, the forensics gal he had been tailing for weeks now: Nikki.

As he passed the assembled group of youngsters, one of them shouted to him. "Hey, you!" He paused for a moment, contemplating his next move, before he sprang towards the youth. Unable to react in time, the young man was pinned against the concrete with a knife to his throat. His friends knew who they were dealing with, and dared not interfere.

"I'm sorry, Mr. Slayer, I didn't know it was you," the boy choked. "I just wanted to spread the news. They're giving out five million dollars to whoever kills the Crimson Arrow!"

The Slayer slowly let his victim go, his heart racing. A bounty - this could be interesting. He'd need to revise the timetable on his target. No matter: she was helpless before him. No, that wasn't right. Helpless *without* him.

He turned back to the group of gangsters sitting idly by. "How would you like to make $5 million, boys?" He sneered and reached for one of his knives. "You can accept, or you can let me set your soul free."

The gangsters looked at each other with puzzled expressions on their faces. Their leader shrugged. "What do we do, Mr. Slayer?"

"Yes," the others echoed. "We're in. Anything you need."

"You boys just sit tight for now. In two days' time, I'll meet you back here with your orders. In the meantime, think about your wish lists."

With a chuckle, he was gone, heading back to his room. His new bride, Nikki, was waiting for him.

"What the fuck are we gonna do about this?" Detective Dustin Roenega of the Mazono Police Department slammed his fist down on the table. His worst fears had just been confirmed: a source in the Backstreets had just called to inform him about the latest developments regarding the Crimson Arrow. He clenched his fists again and let loose a stream of colorful language. He had known that the faceless crime kingpins, the big guys, would eventually come up with a plan to get rid of the Crimson Arrow; he had been dreading this ever since the character had appeared on the scene.

He put his elbows on the table and held his head in his hands. This bounty though: this was extreme. It would bring all sorts of characters into Mazono, all of them hoping to make a quick dollar. He gritted his teeth. No doubt, the crime rate would increase astronomically, and the already overworked and understaffed police force would be forced to deal with the backlash. He groaned as he realized that the coming weeks, maybe even months, were going to be nothing but hell for him and other police officers. He yearned for years past when his job had been easier, fun even.

"Damn you, vigilante scum," he muttered under his breath. "I hope you know what's coming."

Mazono's Maximum-Security Prison housed the worst of the worst. Serial killers and rapists, murderers, drug dealers, and every other category of criminal were kept securely under lock and key. Many times, the guards had been forced to break up a bloody and violent fight between inmates. Before coming to any kind of an understanding, enemy gangs usually engaged in a bitter fight with one another.

Today, the inmates were agog with excitement. Many of them gathered into groups, whispering excitedly amongst themselves. Even the prison officials chatted animatedly as they patrolled in groups. The news of a bounty placed on the vigilante in Mazono had made its way to even these remote quarters, and the inmates were discussing what they would do if they had the freedom to go after him themselves. The guards were wary; a good number of the prisoners seemed more resentful than usual to be in here.

Several of the prisoners outlined elaborate schemes that they were certain could nab the Crimson Arrow. All the discussions ended with a wistful sigh, and the sad realization that they could not escape from here, not even if they tried. The security was just too tight. Normally, it was easy to play the system in Mazono to hit the streets again. Cops and city officials were quite welcoming of bribes. Until you got here, to Maximum-Security. Once you landed here, it was over for you.

While all the other men sat clustered in groups, one man sat motionless in his cell. This man, known as Mr. Goode, listened intently to the news. So, a new vigilante was in town.

Well, well, well, he thought, as a grin widened upon his face. *Well, well, well.*

Two days later, the Slayer chuckled as he paced the floor of the warehouse office. He had set this up perfectly. It had been so easy to manipulate them. All it had taken was one little note to scatter their attention, when the one they were looking to protect had been right under their nose the entire time.

He had finalized his target, captured the prize he'd sought, and enjoyed every second of the time he'd spent with her. His pleasure had mounted minute by minute, second by second, until the ecstatic moment when he released her from her earthly bonds, plunging his knife into her heart.

He rubbed his hands together with glee. Soon he'd have his hands on the detective who loved her and didn't deserve her. The man had had no business trying to interfere in the Slayer's life, and now he would pay for it! First, he'd break the fool's heart and mind, and then he'd destroy his body.

Nikki, even the sound of her name excited him. She'd also been involved in the hunt to find him, yes, but he didn't hold that against her. She'd only been doing her job. It was Zbysko who directed her.

He'd watched Nikki and Detective Zbysko together. Watched how Zbysko ogled her. It was disgusting how the detective coveted the luscious young woman. He chuckled. He had so enjoyed releasing her, so enjoyed the moment when his knife kissed her heart.

He would enjoy the next part of his plan equally.

Nikki was still lying in a pool of blood on the warehouse office floor. He'd clean her up now. He'd lovingly display her on the wall. The first step was to remove the knife and close her wound, the precious wound that had sent her to a better place. The Slayer removed her blouse and bra, pulled out the knife, wiped it and the gash in her breast, then took a needle and thread out of his pocket and cross-stitched the wound closed. Then he removed the rest of her clothing, piece by piece. He threw the bloody clothing in a bag for later disposal.

Delicately, with the love she deserved, the Slayer washed her body. It was a spiritual experience for him. He cleansed it reverently, in precisely the same way he'd have washed Yasmin's had he had the opportunity to do so. When finished, he dressed Nikki in the white lace panties and the veil he'd brought for this purpose.

After applying makeup, loosening Nikki's dark hair from its bun, and brushing it out onto her shoulders, he began the arduous task of affixing her to the wall.

An hour later, covered in sweat from the exertion, he stepped back to admire his work.

She was a beauty! Truly magnificent. Taking a few moments to catch his breath as he enjoyed the spectacle before him, he began to track his next step. He was almost there!

But he had to prepare first. He'd contact one of the hapless idiots who filmed events around the city, trying to make a name for themselves. Men who sought glory would eventually find themselves surrounded by the realization that this world only brought pain and suffering. No one knew that better than him.

He would tempt him with a promise of the "inside scoop" that he so craved. He'd trick him into bringing his next quarry to him by promising him a meeting with the one and only Slayer. To be delivered only if he followed the Slayer's instructions to the letter. He began to laugh. He was building a life's work here. If there were a Pulitzer or a Nobel Prize for serial releasers, he would be a shoo-in.

The Slayer was excited. It was time for the next step.

He walked to the desk, picked up the phone, and tapped in the number. The phone rang five times. He became agitated, shuffling his feet. They had to answer if he hoped to succeed!

"Hello. This is Joey Baker, owner and founder of Maz-TV," a voice finally said, and the Slayer breathed a sigh of relief.

"Listen, here, Baker. I have the scoop of a lifetime for you!"

"I'm listening," Joey said.

"If you want the scoop, you have to promise to do exactly as I tell you!"

"Who is this?" the boy asked, sounding impatient.

"Hey! Don't you use that tone with me! I am the last person you want on your bad side. You don't want to end up displayed on a wall somewhere in town, do you?

"The Slayer ..." Joey said in a tone approaching awe. Then there was a pause. "Hey. How do I know this is really the Slayer and not some stupid prank?" he asked.

The Slayer chuckled. "I guess you'll just have to take my word for it."

"And if I don't?"

"If you don't, you'll lose the biggest story of a lifetime."

"What story?"

"If … and I emphasize the word "if"… you follow my instructions to the letter, I will agree to let you meet me in a secret location and ask me about all the murders I have committed in Mazono. You will get the scoop on the why, the how, and the when."

"And why would you do this? It could get you caught!"

"I will be wearing a mask. I will not give away my identity. I'll meet you in a place where nobody can follow you, where only you and I will know the location."

"Okay," said Joey. "That sounds like a plan …"

"So, do you agree?" the Slayer asked.

"What do I have to do?" the fool asked, the excitement in his voice palpable, and the Slayer knew he had caught a fish. He actually had no plan of following through with what he'd just promised, but he'd had to make it sound real. Apparently, it had done the trick.

The Slayer carefully explained all the details to the reporter wannabe. He promised him the interview at a yet-undisclosed location, in return for the simple task of phoning a certain detective and telling him that the Slayer wanted to talk to him in-person, unarmed, and alone.

Joey was to inform the detective that he would be watched, that Joey had a direct line of communication to the Slayer, and that should the detective appear with any additional persons, the Slayer would be instantly notified, and the arrangements abandoned. Joey would direct the detective where to meet with him. Upon meeting, Joey would ensure the detective had no weapons, or any way of communicating with others. Finally, he'd drive the detective to the Slayer.

Zbysko received the call with a great deal of skepticism. He had vaguely heard of Joey, the reporter for Maz-TV, having watched a few of his broadcasts on various crimes in the city. Joey and his partner were annoying wannabe reporters. He sighed. He guessed everybody had to start somewhere. They were harmless.

Had the boy really spoken to the Slayer, or was someone pulling the kid's leg?

Zbysko shrugged. It wouldn't hurt to find out. It wasn't like he had any better leads on the Slayer right now.

He didn't mind the part about not telling anybody where he was going, because it would actually save him a lot of ribbing if it turned out to be a hoax. But the kid was crazy if he thought a cop would venture into a situation like this unarmed.

Half an hour later, the detective was being dropped off at a warehouse. The kid had asked him if he'd told anybody about this, and he'd said no. Then the kid asked him if he was armed. Again, he'd replied in the negative, holding his arms out to be frisked. "I'll take your word for it," the kid said. Zbysko had counted on that reaction. He chuckled to himself. Frisking a cop would be above the boy's pay grade. He'd have to man up some if he wanted to advance any further in his chosen career.

As Zbysko got out of the car, and practically before he'd shut the door, the vehicle sped off, spraying gravel. Zbysko shook his head and smiled. Kids! All mouth, no balls.

He looked up at the building. Well, if the Slayer were truly here and wanted to talk to him, he'd better get himself inside. His gun was holstered under his arm. He knew the Slayer had a way with knives. Well, if he tried anything, Zbysko would introduce him to his gun.

He entered through a door to a vacant reception area. Then, as directed, he went through another door that led to a set of steps. Nothing seemed amiss yet. He climbed the steps, listening to his own footfalls echoing in the empty stairwell. When he finally arrived at the second floor, he hesitated. Looking across the room, he saw the door to an office where he was supposed to meet the Slayer.

This whole thing was beginning to seem genuine. His pulse quickened. Was he really about to meet the Slayer?

"Hey, you!" Zbysko called.

No answer.

"Come out of there," Zbysko said. "If you dare!"

"Are you armed?" he heard a voice ask.

"No."

"I'll take you at your word. Here I am." With that, a shadowy figure in a ratty overcoat walked out of the door. It was him! The Slayer. Instantly, Zbysko went for his gun.

The figure immediately disappeared back through the door he'd come from. "Come and find me, Detective. I dare you. Or are you afraid to face me without the usual meat sacks beside you for protection?"

"How do I know you're not hiding behind that door with a knife, ready to ambush me?" the detective asked as he advanced toward the door, his gun held in front of him.

"Would that be any way to start our friendly chat, Detective Zbysko?"

In response, Zbysko fired a shot through the door. "Is this friendly enough for you?" he asked.

"My, my. You're not only a pig and a coward, but a liar too."

"Shut up, Slayer, and get out here."

"Oh, but I think you will want to come in here," the Slayer said in a taunting voice. "And see the present I've prepared for you."

"What are you talking about?" the detective demanded.

"Oh, just that there's someone in here that you'd like to see. Maybe if you come in here in time, she'll even survive…" A chuckle.

"Quit the bullshit, Slayer, and get your ass out here."

"Have you seen Nikki today?" the man asked.

"I saw her this morning. She was going to—" Zbysko stopped talking. Oh, my God. No! Without pausing to think, he raced forward, bursting through the door.

A horrific image greeted him. Nikki, the woman he had loved from afar, was pinned to the wall in front of him. Lifeless, wearing a bride's veil. Walt's face contorted with anguish. Then he screamed in rage, searching the room for the monster who had done this.

Too late. A knife flew into the wrist of the hand holding his gun, pinning it to the door frame. A second entered his other arm. The third knife plunged into his left thigh, and the fourth into his right. He was immobilized.

He did not feel the pain yet. All he felt was hatred. If he'd been an animal, he'd have ripped out the man's throat with his teeth.

"How are you feeling now, Detective?" the Slayer asked. "She was beautiful. I so enjoyed releasing her."

"You monster. You piece of shit monster!" the detective screamed. He was losing blood, pinned and crippled, unable to reach his nemesis.

"And I will enjoy this just as much," the Slayer said, as he approached Zbysko. Smiling, he began to carve the man up like a pumpkin on Halloween.

An hour later, the Slayer walked out of the building en route to meet his loose gang of punks. He would have to hurry, because Act Two would start soon.

"So, it's done, finally," Johnny heaved as he looked around him. Barney stood with him, quietly surveying the new surroundings. The two had just finished moving the supplies from the basement to their new base of operations. An older building in the middle of the city, the more central location with various routes in and out would suit their needs well.

They'd convert the main floor into a gym to avert suspicion. The gym would give them a cover for their long absences from social activities, allowing them to work for long hours relatively undisturbed.

That night, Johnny would throw a party to celebrate the opening. He swallowed as a thought came to him.

"You know, April always teased us about our workout routines," he uttered as tears came to his eyes. "Remember how we always joked about opening a gym?"

Barney smiled and nodded. "Yeah, I remember."

"God, I miss her so much," Johnny whispered. Without a word, Barney put a friendly hand on his shoulder, and the two men stood there, both lost in their memories.

Their moment of silence was brief, as the crackling of the police radio caught their attention. Johnny immediately went to change his clothes, while Barney went to his monitors to find out where they were needed.

"There's been an armed robbery. Hollinger Street."

Without a word, Johnny left the building.

When Johnny arrived at the crime scene, the burglars had already taken all they could carry and were leaving the house, warily looking around to ensure that no one could see them.

Johnny immediately hid in the bushes nearest to the home and shot an arrow through the arm of the closest robber. The man fell to the ground, yelling with pain and fear. His partner immediately swore, pulling a gun as he peered into the darkness, wondering where the attacker was hidden.

"I told you this was a bad idea, Frank!" the man on the ground shouted, still clenching his wounded arm.

"Be quiet," Frank hissed as he peered harder, trying to find where the Crimson Arrow could be hiding. He'd heard that the man was able to blend himself into the shadows, but he had thought that those were mere exaggerations. Now he was discovering they weren't.

"I'm bleeding, Frank!" his wounded companion shouted. "Let's get out of here!"

"Not until we have our man," Frank hissed under his breath. A move by the bushes caught his attention, and he ducked, seconds before an arrow went whizzing past him.

"He's in the bushes!" Frank shouted to his friend. "I'm going after him!" With that, he ran towards the shrubbery.

"Come out, you coward!" he shouted. "Come out and face me like a man!"

Cocking his gun, he took aim. There were absolutely no lights here; one would think these rich people would have the sense to put some lights in their yard.

A movement behind the rosebushes caught his attention, and he barely moved in time to avoid another arrow, which grazed his arm.

"Aaaaargh!" he exclaimed, incensed more by the fact that he could not seem to catch the Crimson Arrow than by the wound. He pointed his gun in the direction of the rosebushes and fired. "I'm coming for you, Crimson Arrow, and I am not leaving without you!"

Johnny wondered what that meant. Meanwhile, his pursuer was still breathing threats and abuses, hoping to anger him into making a false move. The criminal was too overcome by desperation and anger to realize that his continued blustering was giving away his position. Johnny stayed hidden, then snuck close enough to get an arrow through the man's leg.

"Motherfucker!" the man exclaimed as he fell. "Look what you did to my fucking leg!"

The Crimson Arrow materialized in front of Frank, looking for all the world like the angel of death. Frank scrambled for his gun, then realized that he had dropped it when he fell. He looked around in a panic, dragging himself backward with the palms of his hands and cursing his unlucky stars. Damnit, he needed that money!

"This what you're looking for?" the Crimson Arrow asked, as he held up Frank's gun. "You won't be needing it anymore," he added, as the sound of sirens drew near.

Frank glared at him. "You think you're so invincible," he spat. "You're about to learn just how mistaken you are."

134

"You're not going to be the one to teach me," the Crimson Arrow replied. Then, pointing to the man's leg, he said, "Don't pull out that arrow. Wouldn't want you to bleed to death." With that, Johnny melted into the darkness.

As Johnny passed through an alley, a sound caught his attention. He stopped and listened. What was that? The sound came again. Static from the coms. Oops. He'd forgotten to turn it on.

Johnny opened his mouth to speak, but before any words could come out, Barney cut him off. "It's him. The Slayer. He's taken another woman. I'm texting you the address now."

Travelling at more than three hundred feet per second, with over 100-foot-pounds of energy, the arrow penetrated the mask and skull of the first gunman just above the bridge of his nose. A tip designed to tear a hole through Kevlar body armor, it sent blood exploding from the point of impact, and took the man's consciousness instantly. A heartbeat later, his unconscious body toppled backward into the room like a building demolition gone wrong...

The second thug heard his friend fall. He cringed. In an instant, his world had gone from happily inconsequential to nightmarish. When the Slayer had told the gang to accompany him and protect this building, he'd thought nothing of it. Now dread swept over him. From the moment the first arrow struck to what seemed a lifetime later, all he'd been able to do was to rise from the couch where he'd been sitting. That, and start a refrain imploring a God whom he'd ignored for years.

Time telescoped again as he screamed, railing at the realization that his opponent was closing in on him fast. His mind responded by rejecting what was happening to him, consigning it to nightmare status.

There was no escape for him though. If this was a nightmare, he wasn't waking.

Fear took total control of his being.

Mumbling, he desperately fumbled for the silver-plated 44 Magnum he'd carried proudly under his arm for years. Clumsy with fear, the thought never entered his mind to seek cover - not that there was much available in the spartan room.

Even as his sweating fingers scrabbled at the slippery ivory butt of his gun, a crimson-clad figure stepped soundlessly through the door, head swivelling, searching for his next target.

Pasty-faced and bug-eyed, the gunman mewled with fear as he came face-to-face with the terror his body had been anticipating.

The Crimson Arrow stepped closer - his mortal enemy was here. These men were just in his way.

Thanks to all the mumbling and scrabbling, the vigilante knew exactly where to find his target even before he stepped through the door. Looking to his left, he saw the fumbling guard trying to get his weapon out of his shoulder holster. The fool never stood a chance.

Mechanical in his precision, the Crimson Arrow wasted no effort, made no grandiose gestures, and took no chances. In a single smooth movement, he turned and fired his arrow. Again, his aim was true.

His hapless target crashed backward into the wall. An abstract artist's splattering of gristle, blood, and gelatinous matter complemented the crimson smear that marked the fumbler's slide down the wall.

The Crimson Arrow neither saw nor heard any other threats as he scanned the area he had just entered. Other than two bodies, the reception area contained a couch, two chairs, and a dirty glass table. An uncompleted game of Rummy was the only legacy left by the blacked-out henchmen.

"Barney, this place is heavily guarded. It doesn't feel right," he whispered.

"Be careful Johnny, it's possible this is a trap. It's not like the Slayer to get tracked down to a location," he said in return.

Looking around, Johnny noticed that the Magnum had never made it out of the holster of his second target. This was going like clockwork; he was in his groove.

Retaining a tight grip on the bow, he made his way quickly and cautiously across the open floor. His destination was one of the two sets of doors at the far end of the reception area. From his quick briefing of the floor plans, he knew that the doors on the right would lead him to the darkened storage area that was supposed to be the heart of any warehouse.

He would exit through those doors and out the back once he was finished in here. Right now, he was headed for the doors on the left. The left-hand doors would open onto some stairs. Those stairs would lead him to the office area on the second floor. The culmination of the vigilante's work would be in those offices. He was almost looking forward to meeting him. They had some pressing business to conclude…

Padding across the green tile floor, his rubber-soled boots did not make a sound. The taut readiness in his body telegraphed his expectancy of further bloody confrontation. A clatter of feet on stairs signalled the approach of reinforcements for the deceased gang members.

Dropping to one knee, he waited for his targets to appear through the left-hand doors. His breathing smooth and even, his body still, he watched the entrance. The bow he held was steady as a rock. Then he caught a flicker of movement through the crack between the swing doors.

"Here we go," he thought as three men burst into the reception area.

The first man's eyes widened as he caught sight of the crimson-clad figure kneeling on the floor. Desperately, he tried to bring his weapon to bear on the man, but he had as little chance of success as his predecessors. His heart quailed as he watched the tip of the vigilante's arrow follow him across the floor.

Pure agony swept through his body as the arrow struck the middle of his chest, pierced his protective vest, and stalled just before penetrating his heart. Slamming his upper body backward, the force jack-knifed his legs up and forwards, imitating a cartoon character.

The second arrow was on its way even before the first came to the end of its journey. Mercifully, the target was out cold before it arrived. Ripping upward through the man's chest at an angle, the second compounded the nearly lethal result of the initial arrow. The man was slam-stopped before his body dropped to the floor.

The second and third men fared no better than the first. Firing at a kneeling target while running full tilt on fancy, leather-soled loafers did not make for accurate shooting. None of the fire directed at the crimson figure came close, as he coolly switched his aim from one target to the next, felling them with precise shots. Seconds later, the skirmish was over, an outcome that would have made any archery coach proud. Even before the echoes of the gunfire died down, the vigilante was up and moving again, this time checking all three men for any signs of life.

As expected, his examination proved that all six shots had been true, his targets were alive. A satisfactory result he felt, bearing in mind that he had been under fire – albeit wildly – while he had been attempting each shot.

Clearly, the arrows had done the job they had been designed to do - the one bulletproof vest had offered no protection against the arrows he had chosen to use tonight. Johnny hadn't known that any of his opposition would be wearing bulletproof vests when he planned this mission, but he lived by the credo of better safe than sorry. The fact that the 'other guys' were lying unconscious on the floor proved the adage to be true.

"They were definitely expecting someone," he murmured.

It didn't make sense for one of these punks to be wearing a vest. The fact that this guy was wearing one signalled the possibility of a storm on the horizon. Had they been expecting trouble of some kind? More to the point – had they been expecting *him*? He could not dismiss the possibility of a prepared defense that was lying in wait for some other threat. *It would be just my luck to walk into some gang-war completely unrelated to the Slayer*, he thought to himself.

He shrugged. It couldn't be helped.

Glancing back at the first body, it suddenly came to him what was amiss: there was dried blood on the man's cuffs. Where did that come from? Bulletproof vests, dried blood – the plot was thickening.

Johnny heard voices behind the swinging doors. He'd have to make a choice – press on, or abandon the operation. Rising, he put all doubts from his mind. This job wasn't over yet, and he was going to finish it, even if he had to fight his way through a third group of thugs.

From the floor plans, he knew that behind those doors was a flight of stairs leading left and up to the second floor of the warehouse, where the offices were located. He had to get up there in double time for this operation to succeed. Those stairs would be the worst place to get caught.

He quickly moved to the doors, unhooking a modified smoke grenade from the webbing on his chest. Waiting beside and behind the doors, with his back to the wall, he heard the clatter of feet rushing down the stairs.

Here they come.

The point-man launched himself down the last few steps, his jacket flapping like a cape behind him. In mid-flight, he encountered a metal object tossed onto the ground at the foot of the stairs. Unable to change his course, the man was blown back by the grenade that erupted beneath his feet. The second man, shielded from the worst of the blast by the first, staggered, bleeding from a myriad of wounds.

After flinging the grenade through the doors, the Crimson Arrow had crouched, turning his head away from the blast. Darting a quick look around the corner now, he searched for any signs of resistance.

"Good timing," he breathed, seeing an unconscious man lying at the foot of the stairs.

Glancing up towards the second-floor landing, he couldn't miss his next target. The staggering, bleeding man held a shotgun. A single arrow was all it took. The man swayed for a moment, and then tumbled down the stairs in a tangle of limbs.

Almost instantaneously, gunfire erupted from the top of the stairs, slamming into the bodies lying at the bottom, and ricocheting off the walls and floor of the bottom landing. Ducking back behind the cover the wall provided, Johnny swore softly. Unless he did something fast, these men would be able to hold him off indefinitely. This was exactly what he didn't want to happen – especially not if this was a chance at catching the Slayer.

This time he swore aloud, instinctively ducking away from the angry buzz of a ricochet skimming over his head. He was still unscathed - but at this rate, his luck was bound to run out sooner rather than later. That had been too close.

"You are not going to live to regret coming here, asshole!" one of the punks yelled.

This was not a time for finesse. Johnny slid a new arrow in place, instantly deciding on a course of action. Turning, he fired blindly around the corner, directing his shot towards the landing at the top of the staircase.

Silence answered. Darting a look around the edge of the wall confirmed to Johnny that there were no moving targets in sight. Rising, he stepped around the corner, keeping his eyes and weapon trained at the top of the stairs.

Stepping carefully near the blood pooling at the bottom of the stairs, he knew losing his footing could be dangerous - and messy. Unfortunately, he couldn't totally avoid the blood as he made his way over the first body. Now he would leave tracks, and the forensic experts would have their first clue. Mentally, he shrugged: that could not be helped. Contrary to movie lore, not all cops were fools. Inevitably, they would find traces of his presence. Those clues would begin accumulating, and soon they would have a thick dossier on him. Still, he would leave them as little as possible to work with. He picked up his enemy's gun, and used the butt of it to distort the tracks that he could. They would have to earn their keep.

Stepping up to the second body, he ripped the shotgun from the hand of its owner and unloaded it.

"Hope you don't mind," he remarked under his breath, "but you don't seem to need it anymore."

The coms buzzed through. "You could've used that, Johnny."

He continued climbing.

Before coming here, Barney had prepped him on the building plans briefly. He even knew how many steps he would climb before reaching the second-floor landing. Below him, the rear doors of the warehouse were locked from the inside. He knew because he had checked. That meant any threats to his health had to come from the room at the top of the stairs, or through the same door he had used to get into the warehouse. The last would only become a factor if he stayed here too long, and he had no intention of being that careless or unlucky.

He needed to hurry. Even if no calls for help could be made from here - he had cut the lines - there would be other lines in nearby warehouses. This ruckus would have attracted attention by now. The police would not take long to respond to reports of a pitched gun battle on the docks. If he were still here when the cops arrived, this could end badly.

Drawing closer to the door at the top of the stairs, he caught a whiff of an unpleasant smell, caused by a reaction often accompanying a violent death.

"That doesn't bode well," he whispered, keeping his eyes on the door.

While he carefully climbed the stairs, a head appeared dead-center in his sights, its owner choosing the worst possible moment to play peek-a-boo.

"Idiot," he thought to himself, as he saw the man's eyes widen in terror. The man's terror did not last very long. Adjusting his aim slightly while still moving forward, Johnny quickly fired three arrows.

Blood and tissue exploded backward into the room at the top of the stairs.

Johnny waited, pressed flat against the wall. Death was playing an ugly symphony in ricochets overhead, but he knew it could not last. This wasn't a movie - bullets inevitably ran out at the worst possible moment. He was happy to wait for that moment to arrive for the men inside the room.

At the first lull in the firing, he slithered forward. Poking around the corner, he snapped three quick shots in the general direction of the gunfire. Bullets again peppered the wall and what was left of the open door, using up precious ammunition.

Ignoring the spray of woodchips, concrete, and other debris raining down on him, Johnny slipped the pin from the stun grenade. Johnny wasn't sure where the men were in the room, but their precise location wasn't important - not when he was using the grenade.

He sent the weapon into the room with a casual backflip of his wrist as he closed his eyes and opened his mouth in preparation.

The remaining defense from inside the room came to an abrupt halt as the stun grenade went off. Even outside the door and with closed eyes, Johnny found the flash and detonation impressive.

Not chancing a quick recovery, Johnny quickly squirmed forward and sighted around the corner, searching for a target. It didn't take long. Seeing movement behind a couch, he fired at it, stuffing exploding from the couch at each impact.

The last man bolted for the office in the corner of the big room, desperation written all over his pale face. Smoothly tracking the moving target, Johnny sighted and fired an arrow. The hapless runner catapulted forward, his head striking the wall of the haven he had tried to reach. Judging from the wet thud on impact and the resulting unnatural angle of the head, Johnny knew he would not have to shoot again.

Quiet descended, the remaining tube of a shattered fluorescent light flashing through the light haze. Bits of couch stuffing floated to the floor as the smell of cordite and blood grew more pronounced.

Striding across the room, he remained alert for any signs of resistance not yet disposed of. None appeared. He turned and headed towards the office the runner had so desperately tried to reach. Somebody was waiting for him in there.

He was cautious as he approached the office, making no sound, and taking care not to frame himself in what remained of the window. Standing to one side, he paused upon reaching the final door, gathering his thoughts, and prepping himself for what lay beyond.

Once ready, he directed a sharp kick at a point just above the lock, crashing the door open.

The sight before him was horrific. Johnny could manage only a brief look at the girl plastered on the wall before turning away. In one corner of the room lay a man's body, slashed to bits. Johnny caught a glimpse of a badge. *Zbysko*. This was the work of the Slayer all right. It was far worse than any turf war between oil-slicked mobsters, or petty shit that ruled the alleys. Johnny's face betrayed little of the anger welling inside him.

"Where are you?!" he called, keeping his back to the wall and his own bow prepped. Silence was his only answer.

"Come out, you monster!" he screamed again.

A soft snicker betrayed the object of Johnny's wrath, and a man stalked into the room, a cold smile playing on his lips.

Johnny stared. Here was the man he had come here for; the one he wanted to get his hands on.

The Slayer.

This piece of shit killed April. Killed the love of Johnny's life. This…this…monster was the reason the person he valued most in the world had been snatched away so cruelly.

With that realization came a red-hot swell of rage. This wasn't the cold, calculating rage that cleared the mind and enhanced logical thinking. This was fiery, volcanic fury that chased out all reason; that eliminated all forms of civility and left only the most primitive of instincts. On the strength of that fury, Johnny let out a roar and charged at the Slayer, throwing him onto the floor. Before the stunned man even had a chance to react, Johnny cornered him and started pounding away at him over and over again, roaring the entire time.

"You bastard! You fucking piece of shit!"

The Slayer raised his hands to protect his face, but it was like being attacked by a wild animal. He had heard that the Crimson Arrow was a rational thinker, a strategist famous for his carefully planned attacks. He had come here planning to counter all his moves, not deal with this mindless creature attacking him.

"You…fucking…disgusting…piece of shit!" Each word was punctuated with heavy punches. "You good-for-nothing murderer! Do you even remember her? Do you even remember her?!"

This immediately registered with the Slayer. He found an opening and managed to dig his knee into Johnny's groin. When Johnny grunted in pain, the Slayer threw him off and stumbled to his feet, breathing hard.

"I guess someone close to you was…released by me?" He laughed, and the sound infuriated Johnny.

"I choose my brides very carefully. I remember all of them," the Slayer continued. "It is gratifying to know that even the mighty Crimson Arrow has benefited from my work." He sniffed and rotated his neck sharply.

"Murderer!" Johnny yelled and charged him again. The Slayer braced himself, but was unable to withstand the onslaught. He fell heavily to the ground, curling into a ball to protect himself from the vicious kicks.

Despite the ferocity of the attack, he rallied himself, grabbed the Crimson Arrow's leg, and pulled. When Johnny fell, the Slayer immediately scrambled to his feet and stumbled away. Blood trickled from the side of his mouth and nose. He wiped it and laughed.

"It feels good, doesn't it? This drive to release, to set someone free. Maybe we aren't so different after all."

"I am nothing like you," Johnny growled, climbing to his feet. He and the Slayer circled each other warily.

"You're just like me," he sneered.

"I do wonder which of them you're talking about?" the Slayer said, mockingly. He had finally formulated a plan. "Was it Serena, the nurse? Or Julia? Very…gifted woman; I was almost sorry to see her go. How about Nikki? You can introduce yourselves now, she's right up on the wall over there. No, no…I'll bet it was April…that feisty lawyer…"

The sound of her name pushed Johnny over the edge, and he lunged at the Slayer again. He was so far gone in his anger that he didn't notice the knife until a sharp pain shot through his side.

"Mmm, April. She was my favorite, you know. That's why I chose not to post her on a wall. Vile creatures like yourselves didn't deserve to view her. I can still taste her blood. It was oh so sweet."

Johnny grunted and jerked away from the knife, managing to move before the Slayer could plunge it deeper. Rather than slow him down, the pain only served to anger Johnny further.

With a cry of rage, he grabbed the hand holding the knife, applied pressure until the grip was broken, and then threw the Slayer over his shoulder. The other man landed hard with a grunt, and immediately began to edge backward, eyes beaming. Johnny pulled the knife out of his abdomen and tossed it aside.

"Not so cocky now, are you?" Johnny said as he walked towards him. The Slayer said nothing, continuing to edge backward until he felt his back hit a wall. Every nerve in Johnny yelled at him to kill, but he intended to savor the moment. He wanted this killer to suffer as April had suffered.

He brought his face close to the fearful, yet defiant killer in front of him. "Yes, this is for April. April Smith. Remember that name. You made the mistake of your life by killing her."

The Slayer laughed. "I didn't kill her; I released her to a higher plane of contentment and serenity. You should be thanking me."

Johnny struck him in the face.

As blood dribbled down the side of his mouth, the Slayer could not help laughing. Even with most of his teeth broken and blood filling his mouth, he laughed, because the almighty Crimson Arrow had lost it.

Kill him. He doesn't deserve to live. Those were the only words running through Johnny's mind as he pulled an arrow from the quiver, fully intending to stab his quarry in the heart. His prey's icy green eyes never wavered from the tip of the arrow.

"It's easy after you've done it the first time," the Slayer grunted, recovering some of his voice. "Now I'll demonstrate."

The Slayer's moves were sudden, but Johnny expected his foe to target his open wound. He countered the knife extending from his opponent's right hand, blocking it perfectly, only to feel a searing pain under his left ribs.

The Slayer's left hand held a second blade.

Fuck. He baited me. Tumbling forward, Johnny fell into the Slayer's knee thrusting upwards, drilling him in the jaw. He flew backwards, dazed.

"You see, Crimson Arrow. You remind me of someone. Someone I hate. For that, I will not release your soul. I will instead torture it."

The Slayer's cackles were drowned out by the noise of Johnny's screams, as slash after slash opened new wounds across his torso. Each cut more painful than the last, he knew he had to act quickly. His torturer refused to let up, joyously swinging blades down upon him.

Johnny realized his only course of action would hurt. As another blade came for him, he opened up his protective stance and allowed it to puncture him, directing it away from his vitals. From there, with both arms free, he used his attacker's momentum to toss him overhead and fling him crashing through the window.

The last blow Johnny received had been the worst, and had gone deeper than expected. He mustered all the strength he had left and gathered himself. Peering out the window, he saw no sign of his mortal enemy.

"Fuck. He got away."

Feeling the rage slowly subside as the agonizing pain he suffered increased, Johnny turned back to the girl on the wall. No human body could sustain such damage and survive. Haltingly and despite his pain, Johnny cut her bonds, rolled her into the fetal position on the ground, and then covered her tenderly with jackets retrieved from the corner of the room, but nothing could hide what had been done to her young body.

Gently, Johnny stroked her hair. He took her hands and squeezed them lightly. Inside, she was only a frightened little girl who fell prey to a monster. This was not the way life was supposed to end for this young woman.

He heard sirens approaching. "I cannot stay" he whispered, "I have to go now."

Adjusting the jackets a final time, he turned to the door.

"Rest in peace," he promised as he left, "I will settle your score as well, Nikki."

As he walked down the stairs, he grew dizzy. He hit the button on his bracelet, but before he could reach the bottom, his body fell, limp.

"Johnny." She looked as beautiful as ever in a flowing white gown that drifted around her like a cloud.

"April," he said, as he tried to gain his bearings. He looked around him. "Where are we?"

She simply continued to look at him, a sad smile on her face.

"Am I dead?" he asked.

She shook her head, never once taking her eyes off him.

He looked around. They were in a beautiful meadow. The sky was blue and clear, the trees were green, the leaves fresh, and the flowers vibrant. The stillness was surreal: there was no air, no movement. However, April's gown continued to float out in all directions, as if caressed by its own private wind.

"I miss you, April." He took a step towards her. Still, she said nothing, but he could see her eyes go moist. "I want to stay here with you."

Silently, she shook her head in response.

"I don't want to go back...please don't make me go back." He increased his pace towards her until he was running. However, no matter how far or how long he ran, he still couldn't reach her.

"April!" he shouted, his frustration getting the better of him. "Please let me stay!"

To his horror, she began to fade into thin air.

"No!" he yelled. "April! April!"

He sat up and looked around, his body sluggish. Cool hands gently pressed him back into the bed.

"Take it easy," Barney's soothing voice said. "It was just a dream."

As the remnants of the agony evoked by the dream faded away, Johnny became aware of the dull pain all across his body and the throbbing of his head, as well as the beeping of an EKG. He winced.

"Take it easy," Barney said again. "You took quite a beating."

Johnny sucked in a deep breath, then winced again as his sides protested. He struggled to keep his heavy lids open, then asked:

"Where…where…am I?"

"You passed out after you turned the tracker on and told me your position. You're in a private ward in the hospital. Pays to be a local celebrity I suppose. I brought you here."

"For…how…how long…have I…"

"Three days. You kept drifting in and out of consciousness, but that's probably because of the drugs they gave you."

"I was….it was…."

"Listen, you can tell me what happened later. Right now, you need to concentrate on getting better."

"How badly…am I …hurt?"

"Well, you have lacerations from head to toe. Luckily nothing major was punctured but you're pretty heavily stitched up. That wound on your left side is particularly sensitive to re-opening. The doctors are confident that you'll heal with time."

"The suit?"

"Don't worry, I have it."

"Okay," Johnny replied. He felt groggy. "I think I need a clothesline arrow. That might help…covering…large…distances. Plus…it would be…pretty cool…"

Barney laughed, "I'll see what I can do. Your parents have already been here to see you. I told them that you got attacked while driving home from work. The best lies come from truth, right?"

Johnny nodded his thanks. He wanted to tell his friend about what had happened, but it was getting harder and harder to stay awake. He struggled to focus on the wall in front of him, and everything was melding into one big, indistinguishable blur.

Hours passed before he came to again. No one was with him in the room this time. Barney must've stepped out to get some food or supplies. Johnny focused on collecting his thoughts.

In his peripheral vision, he noticed someone down the hall walking towards his room. The doctor must be coming to check in.

He'd had the Slayer in his sights. Right where he wanted him. Yet he'd screwed it up by acting on impulse and being overcome with emotion. It'd nearly cost him his life. It wasn't how he'd wanted things to go down, but a valuable lesson was learned in the process. He'd be ready next time.

"Hey doc…"

Johnny turned towards the man entering his room and did not see what he was expecting. The man dressed in what looked like black combat gear was certainly not a doctor. Johnny had no idea who the man was.

"Who are—"

Before the sentence was out, the man flipped over Johnny's bed with one hand, sending him sprawling across the room, his wounds reopening and soaking his hospital gown red. His costume and gear nowhere to be found, Johnny was helpless against the assailant. Who was he? What did he want?

A nurse shot into the room at the sound of the commotion. The man swatted her away, his casual backhand sending her across the room and into the wall. Her imprint remained there as her unconscious body dropped to the floor.

Johnny tried to get up, but the man had already closed the gap and grasped his wrist. His grip was unlike anything Johnny had ever felt. He was completely trapped.

Holding Johnny upright by his wrist, the man studied him the way one would examine a disgusting insect. Seeing Johnny's eyelids flutter, the man knew his victim was fading.

"You're coming with me," he growled, muscles visibly rippling beneath his clothing in readiness of physical activity.

He dragged Johnny's body through the room and into the hallway, by now filled with personnel who had heard the commotion and were trying to impede the intruder's path.

The man shrugged off the nurses who tried to stop him as if they were weightless.

"Hold it right there," a voice said.

The hospital security guard never stood a chance. With his free hand, Johnny's captor pulled out a gun and put a bullet in the guard's leg, spewing blood on his once pristine uniform.

Stay conscious, Johnny. If you want to stay alive, stay conscious.

Hospital staff hurried out exits or hid behind patients' doors.

Placing the gun back in its holster, the man carried Johnny's body down the stairs. Leaving through the back doors, he tossed Johnny into the rear of a van.

Barney heard the commotion from across the road, and witnessed the mass exodus of people from the front of the hospital. This couldn't be good. He hurried toward Johnny's room, only to find his friend missing, blood and debris everywhere.

Johnny would be vulnerable, coming off painkillers and recently wounded from last night's attack. Barney rushed to the front desk, which had been abandoned. He found the camera watching Johnny's room and quickly replayed the attack. Then he switched cameras and saw his friend being loaded into a van.

It was too late to chase after the van, although he wanted to. He needed to think. When he replayed the video feed, two things stood out. First, this man had had a perfect opportunity to kill Johnny then and there. He didn't, so there must be some ulterior motive or need to keep him alive. Second, the manner in which the man approached the situation made it likely that he knew Johnny was the Crimson Arrow. Both of these things concerned Barney. The best he could do for now was to get back to the warehouse, figure out what was going on, and start tracking the van's movements.

Before driving off, the man felt Johnny's pulse.

Still kicking. Good.

He hopped in the driver's door and sped away, accelerating rapidly. He had no urge to keep his captive any longer than necessary. He wanted to deliver him, collect what he was owed, and get out of town.

In the back of the van, Johnny slowly regained consciousness. Where am I? What's going on? He blinked his eyes several times, then noticed the sensation of motion. He must be in a vehicle of some sort.

What vehicle? How? Thinking back as hard as he could, the last thing he remembered was being in the hospital, where a huge brute attacked him. After flinging Johnny across the room onto the floor, the man picked Johnny up by his wrist as if he were a feather's weight. He'd then drug Johnny down the hospital corridors, shooting people as he went. Johnny remembered desperately trying to stay conscious. Then he must've passed out.

Johnny looked down at himself. His hospital gown was soaked in blood. As if triggered by the sight of his own blood, Johnny's wounds began to sting and burn. He groaned and held his side. His wounds had opened. Hopefully, he wouldn't bleed to death before getting out of this situation.

There had to be a way out of here. He studied his surroundings. He appeared to be on the floor of what looked like the interior of a van. The van was empty except for Johnny, and what looked like rolled-up carpet piled against the walls on either side.

Could things get any worse? Yes, he told himself. He could be dead. As it was, he was still alive. That was about the only positive he could find in his current situation. *Which was?* He asked himself again. Unbelievable at best. He almost smiled at the absurdity. He, the Crimson Arrow, dressed in nothing but a hospital gown, was being kidnapped by an oaf in combat gear who possessed superhuman strength. What next?

Sunlight was streaming into the van through high, small windows on either side. Johnny was just about to get to his feet and test what he could see out of the van's windows when from out of nowhere, an explosion shook the vehicle. The van swayed haphazardly, narrowly avoiding other cars. It careened from one side of the road to the other, either because it was damaged, or because the driver was injured.

Johnny curled into a ball to protect himself as he was thrown willy-nilly around the van's interior. When it finally appeared that the van was going to right itself, another vehicle smashed into it. The van spun wildly before toppling onto its side.

Johnny struggled to look through a window, trying to understand what he was seeing, when a deafening blast erupted from the vehicle next to them, sending Johnny flying backwards across the van. Still groggy, he was able to notice two things. First, his assailant's gun lay on the ground near him. Second, he was still wearing his bracelet.

Before he could regroup, another explosion knocked the breath out of him. As he fought to remain conscious, he heard someone laughing. He quickly hit the button on his wrist. The man who had abducted him was out cold in the front seat. Grabbing the man's gun, Johnny struggled to make his way to the back doors of the van.

Pushing the doors open, Johnny all but fell out of the van. He crawled to the van's side, his face and entire body now soaked in blood, then collapsed flat on the ground. Through a haze, he made out the shadow of a figure approaching.

Am I going to die? Johnny looked up. Standing before him was a stocky man with long black hair.

"Well hello, Mister Crimson Arrow," the man said, grinning. He had a thick accent, but Johnny couldn't place it. "I've always been one for grand entrances, and I really pulled this one off, don't ya think?" He watched with amusement as Johnny struggled to get to his feet and wipe the dust out of his eyes.

"Allow me to introduce myself. My name is Victor Sheath, the baddest fooker you'll ev'r meet." He bowed low, then straightened up and fixed Johnny with a thoughtful look.

"I must say though, I rather thought you'd be, I dunno, bigger? Scarier? Ya look pre'y ordinary to me. Perhaps it's the lil' gown yer wearing." The man paused to chuckle.

"Oh no, ya don't," he said when Johnny reached for the gun. Victor Sheath held up what was in his hand - it looked like a remote of sorts - and pushed a button. Immediately, another blast erupted as the man laughed with glee.

"Isn't it great?" he asked, as Johnny continued trying to climb to his feet. "Ya want to know what I did? I rigged the entire area with explosives. These lil' balls are a work of genius, I tell ya. I just need to point in your direction and hit the button. That er make one collide with somethin' at a high impact and BOOM. It's actually pre'y humane if you ask me. No point in killing er'yone when yer after just one person. Not that I mind an accidental killin' or ten."

Johnny rose, holding his side. He was breathing heavily, his legs were shaking, and his head was pounding from the blow it took from the last blast. He took deep, measured breaths as he tried to make sense of this madman in front of him. Who was he? He said his name was Sheath. Victor Sheath. The name meant nothing to Johnny. One thing was clear, though. He had walked into a trap, and this man fully intended to play with him for as long as possible before finally killing him. He had to get out of here as soon as possible. He didn't know how much more punishment his body could take.

"I think you have the wrong guy."

Sheath's eyes twinkled. "Do I now?"

"Yes. I'm not this Crimson Arrow or whoever it is you're looking for."

"I s'pose that's possible. Yer not in costume after all. Then again…"

Another explosion went off and blew Johnny completely off his feet.

"Ol' Scooter o'er there wouldn'ta taken ya if ya weren't the genuine article."

Johnny, lying on the ground, slowly glanced towards the front end of the car.

"Don't ya worry. I've been doing this a long fooking time. I made sure he was out before I made my way ov'r. Trackers. Let me tell ya. They do all the findin' and yers truly swoops in to do the collectin'."

Sheath kept talking. "I get what yer trying to do, boy, I really do. It's just that, well, it's all so futile! What, ya think yer going to single-handedly put an end to crime? In this pile o' shit city? Yer fooking mad." he laughed. "It's fooking mental for anyone to think they can change a damn thing here. Live and let live, I always say." He burst with sudden laughter.

"Yes, live and let live's my motto. Except for when I have to, ya know, kill someone. Unfortunately, yer next on my list."

While Sheath was talking, Johnny took deep, slow breaths and deliberately steered his thoughts away from the pain in his sides, his back, and his head.

He had to rise above the pain, or this madman would blow him into tiny bits. He tried to remain calm and assess the situation. It was no use. *I can't do this. He's ten steps ahead of me. I'm going to die.*

Tears streamed down Johnny's cheeks. His body, worn as it was, shook. Thoughts of April filled his head. Is this how she felt? Had she feared death at the hands of the Slayer?

No, he decided. She'd been strong. Stronger than he was. She'd have kept fighting.

Johnny, on the other hand, couldn't. Doubt and fear and lodged in his mind. Emotionless, he resigned himself to his fate. He was as good as dead.

"Tears, really? Yer a disgrace." Sheath spit on the ground in front of him.

"I was plannin' on draggin' this out a bit, but I won't be toleratin' no squirly cryin' fook."

Just then, an arrow came whizzing by Sheath's head. Head on a swivel, he spun around. Standing down the road was the Crimson Arrow.

"Looking for me?" the man donning the Crimson Arrow costume said.

"Matter a fact I was," Sheath replied.

What's going on here? Did Scootsy fook up? Nah. This one had me dead to rights and missed. This is…a distraction. Fook.

Sheath dove down to one side and hit the ground, narrowly dodging the bullet shot from behind him. Johnny had seized the opportunity of the man's distraction to grab the gun and shoot. With all the strength he could muster, Johnny bolted towards the nearest alley.

As Sheath tried to rise, another arrow flew over his head. He frowned, glowering. His captive was nowhere in sight now – but he couldn't have gone far. Meanwhile, Scooter wouldn't be out much longer. That wouldn't be a favorable fight. Plus, who knows who else got the memo? Without a strategy, he was cooked. The imposter was still visible down the road, but at that distance he was no threat.

Sheath sighed. "Me and my big fooking mouth." Then he squeezed hard on his remote. One after another, explosions hit, engulfing the area in flames. The ground shook, and Sheath himself stumbled. Smoke surrounded the area.

Meanwhile, Johnny had created distance between himself and his two attackers. He needed somewhere to hide; somewhere he could blend with the shadows. This street was too open; Sheath would find him in a heartbeat. If what he said was true, Sheath could blow up the whole neighborhood in an instant. Unless Sheath was truly a madman though, he wouldn't go that route before finding his target.

With that thought in mind, Johnny stumbled to an alley at the end of the road. It wasn't much, but it was all the cover he had. Thankfully, he didn't need to find Barney. Barney would find him.

Johnny staggered on, holding his sides, focusing every thought, every ounce of energy, on putting one step before the other. He had to get out of here. Then the sky brightened, and everything was engulfed in flames. Surrounding buildings lit up, and the shockwaves sent him soaring against a dumpster.

"Johnny, stay with me."

Groggily, he came to at the sound of the familiar voice. His eyes fluttered open to find his arm was around Barney, as he was being led through another alley. Barney was still in the Crimson Arrow suit.

Darkness was taking over the sky. Barney led Johnny around a corner. They were in a sketchy part of town now. Finding a spot that looked unoccupied, Barney kicked in the door, then laid Johnny on the floor against a wall.

"My car was blown up in the explosions. Sorry, but we're going to have to get out of here on foot."

The two men laid back and rested.

"Thanks, Barn. You had my back."

"Always. Who was that guy?"

"He said his name was Victor Sheath, and he called the guy who'd thrown me in the van Scooter. Sheath definitely wanted to kill me. Scooter definitely tried to take me. I'm a target."

"We've got to get someplace safe as soon as we can."

"Just let me rest a bit more," Johnny said. "I was sure I was done back there until you showed up."

"You need to get out of that gown and clean yourself up. You look ridiculous," Barney laughed.

Johnny looked down at himself and laughed too. "You need to get out of my suit and let me put it on."

"I thought you'd say that," Barney said, and pulled a change of clothes out of a bag. "I'll take the gun, please," he added.

Barney had also brought some bandages, which he wound around Johnny's side to help hold his knife wound closed and slow the bleeding down.

The men stayed silent, catching their breath and sharing the bottle of water Barney had brought along. They'd wait until full dark before making their move.

When the light had totally faded, Johnny got to his feet. "Time to move," he said.

"Any idea of what we're heading into?" Barney asked.

"Something close to hell, I'd reckon."

"I'm glad it's you they're after, not me," Barney said and grinned.

"You would be," Johnny replied.

"Seriously, do you have any idea what we're going to do to get out of this? Those characters are straight out of a nightmare. One has superhuman strength. The other blows everything in sight up. I mean, what next?

"I don't know. I'm afraid to find out. I don't think this was what we had in mind when we decided to avenge April."

"And to clean up the city the way she wanted to."

"Right."

"Well, time to go. Ready?"

"Yeah."

They ran into the open clearing, and Johnny made out the faint outlines of a crumbled building half-destroyed by an explosion. They sidestepped into the shadows. It was too dangerous to walk in the lights. The Crimson Arrow was a large cake, and everyone wanted a piece of him.

Johnny had taken only three measured steps in the darkness, when hard metal slammed into his shoulder. He moaned as he crashed to the ground. Barney stood a few feet away, silent.

"Hello, Crimson Arrow," a cold, emotionless voice said. Johnny was certain he'd heard it before. "Your crusade ends here and now."

The figure towered before Johnny, a gun aimed at his head, like a villain from a comic book, eyes seething, nose flaring as he breathed. Yes, he knew him. He was the man who had been at the scene of the first crime he had stopped.

It was Detective Dustin Roenega of the Mazono Police Department.

"Make one move," Roenega said as he aimed the police issued .9mm pistol squarely at Johnny, his expression stern and calculated, his body rigid. "Make one silly move, and you're done," he finished as his jacket billowed behind him in the night breeze.

"Officer," the Crimson Arrow said, "I am not the enemy here."

"You are according to my book, and by the casualties credited to you." Roenega's index finger was gingerly pressed against the hammer of the weapon. He didn't want to take any chances. Surprisingly, the vigilante wasn't making a break for it.

"Look," the Crimson Arrow said, losing his patience. "The real bad guys caused this mess, not me!" He tilted his head toward the site of the explosions. "Innocent people are injured, or worse, dead," he continued. "The city needs to be salvaged. They need to be saved. Go save them."

Johnny tried to stand up, but the barrel pointed at his head dissuaded him.

"And you need to be put behind bars," Roenega said.

"How's that going to solve the current situation?"

"Probably won't. But this whole disaster is because of you, and I'm sure as hell gonna feel good knowing I've put the Crimson Arrow away for good."

Suddenly, fire lit up the night sky.

Johnny pointed. "See, Detective, those people need saving, and if you waste your time on me, then their blood is on you."

The words seemed to affect the detective, and his aim faltered briefly.

Sometimes, Roenega blamed himself for the unsolved cases, their files gathering dust in storage. The guilt birthed of his unwillingness to push the limits and solve those cases enveloped him every night in bed. Sometimes, he could hear the victims' voices in his sleep. The Crimson Arrow might be partially right. But he wasn't letting him off that easy. He lowered his aim, so that the pistol was now directed at Johnny's chest, hovering close to his thumping heart.

"Who the hell made you judge, jury, and executioner?" Roenega asked.

"Let's not get in over our heads here, Detective."

"Correct me if I'm wrong, but the Mazono PD didn't hire you to do our jobs."

"Your jobs?!" Barney chimed in. "Mazono is overrun by criminals and drug barons! What has the precinct done to protect the citizens?"

"I—I..."

"Nothing! Homicides keep happening, and nothing is done to solve the problem. Nothing!" Barney declared.

"But this crusade—" Roenega objected.

"Yeah, well, I agree my methods have been unorthodox, undiplomatic, and old-fashioned," Johnny said. "But in the end, it has gotten shit done. Results are the only thing that matters right now as far as I'm concerned." Johnny sprang to his feet, half-stunned that the detective hadn't sent a bullet into his chest. He fixed his eyes on Roenega, whose hands were now shaking.

"Look, Detective, you've got two options: you can either put that weapon away, and salvage what's left of this neighborhood and its inhabitants, or you can go right ahead and pull the trigger."

After what seemed like an eternity, the detective gave a resigned sigh, and tucked the weapon away in his holster.

"Thank you, Detective. You're a good man."

"Don't be so sure of yourself," Detective Roenega warned, almost to himself, "I'm going to take you in someday."

Ashley Hayes sat on a stool in a bar on Franklin Street, the seediest part of town next to the Backstreets.

"What's going on?" she asked.

The place was deserted except for Ashley, her informant, and the bartender who was cleaning glasses at the far side of the bar. It was too early for the clientele to come in, but Ashley knew that once the sun set, the place would become a madhouse.

Her informant had insisted that they meet here, afraid that they would be seen together if they met in the Backstreets. Even now, he sent furtive looks over his shoulders and kept pulling the bill of his cap lower and lower over his face. He was beginning to freak her out.

"Gavin, what's wrong? Nobody can find you here, you know." And that was another thing. This mysterious "they" that Gavin kept referring to over and over again, but wouldn't identify.

"Gavin." She leaned over and took his hand to get him to focus on her. He had been reluctant to talk to her, but the lure of her monetary offer had proven too strong to resist.

"Gavin. Tell me what you know," she urged.

After peering around for a few more minutes, he finally settled his gaze on her.

"They want him dead," he said finally, after taking a deep swig of his beer.

"Who?"

"The big guys. They want the Crimson Arrow dead. They killed my boss over a disagreement about the methods."

Ashley was confused. She had noted the increased rate of crime and criminal activities in Mazono City in the past few days, and had decided to investigate it for her paper. In the course of her investigation, she had decided to contact Gavin, her trusted informant from the Backstreets. What she hadn't expected was this near terror he was exhibiting.

"Why?" she asked.

"He's ruffling the feathers of the elite," Gavin replied. "So, they've placed a huge bounty on his head. It's crazy. Even the big guns have come to take him down."

That sounded interesting. "Is that why violence has been on the rise in the past few days?"

He nodded. "Things are about to get much worse before they get better. These people won't have any problem destroying the city to get the job done."

Finally, they'd made it back to home base. Johnny began taking off the suit, as Barney grabbed some medical supplies from a cupboard. He helped Johnny clean his wounds and get patched up.

Johnny grabbed an ice pack and lay down on a couch in the corner. His head was throbbing. He tried to remain as still as possible to keep his many wounds from opening up.

The two men rested in silence.

Finally, Barney grabbed his laptop to turn on the news. It seemed that the explosions had been dealt with. *Thank God.* There were casualties, but the situation appeared to be contained.

"I think you should rest. I should too. It's been a long day. We need to recoup," Barney said.

"Agreed."

Johnny fell into a much-needed slumber, the pain disappearing as he drowsed.

Johnny awoke in the middle of a beautiful meadow. The colors were vibrant, and the breeze gentle. The sun had reached the perfect peak. This was a happy place.

"Hello, my love," rang a familiar voice. Johnny rose and whirled around. There was April. As beautiful as ever.

"I've missed you, April." Tears formed in Johnny's eyes as he spoke.

"I've missed you too."

"Life is so hard without you. I'm a wreck."

"Johnny, life is always hard. You have to persevere."

"That's easy for you to say. You're stronger than I am. You fought for what you believed in. For what was right."

"So have you, Johnny."

"Me? Fought? I was handed everything. I freeze when things get tough. I froze and lost you. I'm not strong at all." Johnny felt shame. He had never deserved April. Still, he couldn't take his eyes off of her now. He yearned to savor every moment in her presence. If he could keep her in his sight, maybe this time she wouldn't go, wouldn't die.

"If you aren't strong, how have you kept on with this fight?" she asked. "What has kept you hunting my killer and protecting our city? A weak person wouldn't do that. They couldn't!" she exclaimed.

Before Johnny could respond, a loud noise in the distance caught his attention. It was repetitive, and coming closer. What was it? An alarm?

An alarm rang throughout the building. Johnny woke up and looked around, regretting being pulled out of his dream. "What's going on?" he asked.

Barney checked his laptop. The bottom of the screen was flashing. He clicked the icon and it tapped into a camera.

"What is that?" Johnny asked.

Barney sat still, looking at the film wide-eyed. It was coming from their old operations center, the basement of Johnny's father's building.

The man who'd kidnapped Johnny from the hospital was there. The door had been smashed through as though a truck had rammed it. The man was rummaging through everything he could find, destroying equipment and furnishings seemingly without effort. He was searching for something.

"Johnny..." Barney said, "He found our old base."

Johnny stayed silent.

Barney looked over at his friend, who had gone pale and was trembling. Then he looked back to the screen and saw that the man had found the video camera they were now looking through. Could the man find them here?

The TV in the corner flashed an announcement. A live video feed of the Backstreets came up on the screen, and Barney sat in awe at the sight of the destruction: the entire area had been reduced to rubble.

The pavement was painted red with the blood of victims unfortunate enough to be present during the bombings. The luckier ones were being carried out in stretchers, as the fire department hosed down a burning building. As Barney watched, a car exploded, and several bystanders were blown backward. They scattered on the ground, unmoving.

The police radio also went off. Johnny groaned as he realized that the dispatcher was calling all units available to the Backstreets and the surrounding area, where a series of explosions had destroyed more buildings.

"We're in a lot of trouble," Barney said. There was no response. He turned around and saw Johnny heading for the door.

"Where are you going?" Barney asked, returning his stare to the laptop's screen.

"I'm leaving. I can't go out there and it looks like we can't stay here either."

"What do you mean you're leaving?" Barney said, louder than before. "You're going to give up? Now? You're going to run away like a coward?"

"That's exactly what I'm going to do. I am a coward." Johnny had reached the stairs.

"April was wrong about you."

Johnny's body froze.

"What'd you say?"

"You heard me."

Johnny swung around and strode over to Barney. "Say it again," he said as he shoved his friend, blood trickling from a freshly re-opened wound.

"If this is who you are, April was wrong about you and I wish I had never given you my permission to marry her."

The next thing he knew, Barney was on the ground, face red and seething with pain. He'd been struck in the face.

Johnny bellowed his hatred into the air, then spent, began to sob.

"We have to do something," Barney pleaded.

Johnny let himself fall to the floor next to his friend. "What?! What can we do?! You know that when the going got tough, I always quit or froze! I can't stop them…and I don't want to die…" Johnny said in a hoarse voice.

"Look, I don't know what to do either, Johnny. But this was the mission we decided to take. We can't let this city be destroyed. There are good people out there. Cleaning up Mazono was something we agreed upon together. That's the vow we made." He cleared his throat.

"You don't have to tell me that!" Johnny said.

"I know we're not prepared for something like this. I know that if you go out there, you may die. I lost my sister. My family is broken. I can't lose you too…I can't."

Johnny covered his face with his hands, hiding the tears streaming from his eyes.

"But I can't live with the regret of letting these people die either. April believed you were strong. She didn't care that you froze up in your MMA fight. She didn't care that you'd get in your head when things didn't go your way. Because she knew that if she were ever in danger, you would overcome that and protect her."

Johnny sobbed, on the verge of breaking down.

"A few days before she died, April told me the story of her date gone wrong and being attacked in the Backstreets. You saved her. She told me she made you promise not to tell me. She was so grateful to you for saving her. And for keeping it a secret until she was ready to tell me. "

"Yeah, and then she died because I *couldn't* protect her." Johnny spat.

"You can't keep torturing yourself like that. The damage was done by the time you showed up. If you insist on blaming yourself, then make sure what happened to her doesn't happen to anyone else. You can still honor her that way. That's what she would want. It's what the Judge would have done. I believe in you. I'm not going to ask you to do anything I'm not willing to do myself. I'm with you one hundred percent."

Johnny dropped his hands from his face and straightened his back. "You're right," he said. "That is exactly what she'd want. But what if I freeze up again? I'm dead if that happens."

"If your response was to freeze, you wouldn't have been able to do the things you've done. You didn't freeze against the Slayer. You did the opposite. You didn't know if you could win, but you went for it anyway."

"I'm not sure I can do this, Barn."

"You can do it."

"What makes you think I can do it, when I don't?"

"I know you Johnny. You're my best friend. I know you better than you know yourself. You look at yourself through a lens of self-doubt. I look at you through a lens of reality. April saw the man you are, and I see it too. I believe in you, Johnny!"

Johnny nodded, as he realized Barney's words were true. "You're right. By letting my self-doubt rule me, I've been my own worst enemy. Still, we need to navigate this carefully."

"Agreed, we need a plan. If we go out there and wing it like usual, we're dead. These people are all professionals. We also need to be careful of the fact that we don't know how many there are."

"You're telling me there could be more? I didn't even think about that," Johnny said, now rubbing his painful sides.

"Yes, Sheath is trying to lure you out. However, with all the commotion, his efforts are sure to have gotten the attention of the others. The man who kidnapped you, the Slayer himself, and God knows who else. We need help."

"Help," Johnny repeated, wracking his brain for any idea that might be hiding there.

"Yes, help."

Suddenly, Johnny spoke. "I've got an idea. I need you to stay here and man the video cameras like your life depends on it. Mine does. Find Sheath for me. Don't worry, the coms will be on when needed. I need to make a phone call. Can you transmit my bracelet data remotely?"

Barney nodded. "I can."

"Okay."

Barney looked at his friend, holding his gaze. "I know you don't want to hear this, but it needs to be said. With these guys, if the opportunity presents itself...you have to go for the kill. There's no holding back if you want to survive. And I need you to survive."

Johnny nodded once, then picked up the suit and his bow.

"Oh, and you'll need this."

Johnny smiled, "You rat bastard."

"All units," Detective Dusty Roenega of the Mazono Police Department barked into the coms device firmly grasped in his palm, hard lines streaking his pallid face. "Get in position. We're moving out."

What the hell? Roenega pondered, as he strapped the coms back to his hip. Mazono had turned into a deadly hail of fire and catastrophe in a matter of seconds. Everything was spiralling out of control. On Roenega's teakwood desk sat his desktop transmitting live footage from Maz-TV, an amateur YouView streaming outlet that prided itself on being 'first on the scene.' He found out that the Backstreets had suffered from massive explosions, many inhabitants were feared dead, and a greater number were unaccounted for.

In the live feed, a woman cradled the mangled remains of a child, the horror on her face visible as she threw back her head in anguish. This stunned Roenega momentarily.

Unbelievable. All this destruction.

"The death toll in the last few minutes," the wannabe reporter, a young boy dressed in a polo shirt and messy jeans, was saying when an explosion rocked a building nearby. The ensuing blast drowned his words, throwing everyone around and distorting the live video feed. When the dust cleared away, and the feed came back into focus, a massive concrete slab sat atop the woman who'd been holding the child, her legs extending out from beneath it.

"Ian, are we still live?" the reporter asked in hushed tones as he struggled to his feet.

"Yeah. We're good." The voice behind the camera was airy, almost breathless. The video jittered for a bit, then swarmed back into focus. "We're gonna have a truckload of subscribers after this."

"Hell, yeah." The reporter appeared on the screen, his hair now a tangled mess of dust and particles, his shirt rumpled beyond recognition. "The death toll," he repeated, staring head-on into the camera, "in the last few minutes has surpassed the numbers of any event in Mazono in the last 30 years. My heart and prayers are with the families of those who've been wounded." He paused, taking a moment to fix his gaze squarely on the giant pile of concrete and the pair of legs poking out. "Or killed," he added. "We can only hope that the Police and the Crimson Arrow, that fearless vigilante, swing into action and save the day. Er … night."

"That's good, Joey," the voice behind the camera whispered. "You're doing great."

"My name is Joey Baker, and this is Maz-TV! Always first on the scene. Subscribe to our channel to get more breath-taking videos and amazing interviews, all from the ill-fated city of Mazono, and we'll keep you updated as often as possible," he finished. The video feed was severed immediately.

Joey was relieved. After the disaster when he ended up inadvertently getting Special Agent Zbysko murdered, he didn't think he could face another failure. Even though nobody ever found out what had led the detective to the spot where the Slayer killed him, Joey's conscious weighed heavy.

He kept telling himself that all he'd done was relay a message, so it hadn't been his fault, really. Unfortunately, he had trouble believing that one hundred percent. He'd also found out that the Slayer had never had any intention of granting him an interview, and had just used him as a pawn in his game. This here though, tonight, was going exceptionally well. In his own eyes at least, Joey might redeem himself yet. He smiled.

Sheath is a madman, Johnny thought as he made his way through the streets. A madman who seemed to delight in death and destruction, and was obviously ruthless, judging by the level of chaos he had unleashed on the city in a bid to draw his quarry out. As Johnny headed toward Merrick Street, he tried to plan his attack against Sheath. The first thing Johnny had to do was get that damned remote. He had no doubt that there were still more bombs hidden strategically and waiting to be detonated. He didn't want a repeat of the last time he had faced Sheath.

In the darkness, he could easily move without being seen. Barney had done a wonderful job wrapping his wounds up tight. He'd also had much practice blending with the darkness, and now he moved as one with it. Nobody was going to find him, unless they were specifically looking for something or someone in the shadows.

He walked briskly, almost running, as he slipped from shadow to shadow, unseen, unheard, and without engaging a single person until he neared the chaos.

"Ian, Ian, we still good?"

"Yeah, yeah. Go on, Joey."

The lanky youth stared into the camera, trying very hard to replicate the grave-faced, professional journalists who he had seen reporting sad news. It was a fight to keep the expression on his face professional, while he was struggling with excitement. He and the cameraman were the first on the site of chaos, and it seemed they were still the only ones reporting the disaster live.

Ian moved the camera to show a man in the ruins, holding what appeared to be a limp, bleeding woman, possibly dead. The shock in his eyes was heartbreaking. He wasn't screaming, wasn't speaking, just standing there, holding what might be his wife or might be a stranger, and looking lost. He was the picture of the city, Mazono, which had been brought down to her knees. The camera shifted to the burning buildings, taking in one after the other before it finally returned to the wannabe reporter.

"This is Joey Baker, reporting live from Mazono."

Johnny's feet thudded on the road, his body lithe and wiry as he ran winding between abandoned junk thrown haphazardly in the alleyway. Johnny sprinted as fast as his legs could carry him, his mind racing with thoughts.

Since the day Barney and he decided to embark on this crusade of cleansing Mazono of evil, he'd never felt like prey before. It had always been he himself on the prowl, dismantling his enemies before they even understood what was unfolding around them. Now, the tables had turned, and he was the prey that the hunters wanted to take out by any means necessary.

The Slayer. Scooter. Victor Sheath.

Johnny surveyed the scene. The screens back at the lair showed only a fraction of the devastation now encompassing the area. Fires ran rampant across the destroyed buildings, and smoke filled the air like a loathsome fog.

Johnny found cover in an alley. He needed to stop and think. Running around in plain sight was a death wish. Thankfully, the smoke would act as perfect cover.

Another explosion fired off in the distance. He started moving toward the chaos ahead.

"Help!" a tiny voice screamed through the roar of the flames.

The Crimson Arrow's head turned towards the direction of the cry. He moved fast and found himself before a wall of fire instead of the door that was supposed to be there. Gritting his teeth, he dove through it.

Quickly scanning the area, he found no sign of life.

"Help!" the voice came again.

The sound was coming from the next floor up. Johnny ran up the stairs and paused again, listening.

"Help."

There it was. Coming from behind a closed door. He tried the handle. Locked. With a grimace, he threw his shoulder against the door. As it gave way beneath his weight, Johnny stumbled into the room.

The fire burning outside and around the house barely illuminated the inside of the room. Johnny held still until his eyes adjusted to the semi-darkness. A little boy sat curled up in a back corner.

"Hey buddy. Let me get you out of here," Johnny called. The boy's eyes found the Crimson Arrow and lit up.

Immediately, the lad leaped to his feet and ran to Johnny, who pulled the boy into his arms. Johnny noted how fragile the child felt.

"You ready?" he asked the boy.

"What about the lady?"

"What lady…"

The snap of a whip echoed across the room before coiling itself around Johnny's neck. The whip tightened around his throat, suffocating him as he struggled against it. He lost his footing, nudging the boy towards the collapsed door as he fell backwards.

"My hero," said a sneering woman behind him. "Run along little boy," she said. "The adults are going to play." She punctuated each sentence with a tug on the whip, keeping Johnny from regaining his balance.

The little boy ducked around the corner, peeking back at them, seemingly hesitant to go farther.

I need to keep him safe, Johnny told himself. He grabbed the whip and pulled. As the woman stumbled across the semi-dark room, he freed his neck from her whip.

"Using a child as bait, you're disgusting," he said, glaring at her.

"It worked, didn't it?" she crooned, running her hands up and down her tightly latex-clad thighs. Johnny sensed she was trying to distract him and remained alert.

"What, you don't like?" she asked.

"Where's Sheath?"

"I'm not enough for you? How insulting."

He was beside her before she could accustom her eyes to his movement.

This guy is quick, she thought, eyeing the arrowhead trained on her forehead.

"Where's Sheath?" Johnny spat.

"You don't need to worry about anyone but me, darling. Alana is here to take care of you."

With that, her left fist connected with Johnny's face, sending him stumbling back into the darkness. His arm swirled blindly in response before Alana's head scissors took him straight to the ground.

He jumped up fast, dodging a blow from her as he did so and punching her in the stomach. She did not let him finish with his combination, countering with a jab of her own. He dodged it and struck at her face multiple times in quick succession.

Blinded, she stumbled, then quickly recovered her feet and rushed toward him.

He heard her grunt the instant before he felt a sudden pain in his gut. She twisted and turned her knife, eliciting a bout of pain Crimson Arrow never imagined existed. He leapt back to create some distance between them.

"I'm sorry, did that hurt?" she whispered through her bloodied face.

A shiny ball flew through the smashed-out window. The Crimson Arrow saw it reflected in Alana's eyes. His heart dropped as he remembered the boy.

His instincts kicked in, stronger than the pain he felt. He dove toward the door, grabbed the boy, and dashed to the other side of the building, hoping to shield the child from the blast.

Chest heaving in and out and sweat darkening his costume, Johnny raced to an open window.

The ground looked a long way down.

"Hold me tight!" he asked the boy, not waiting for an answer.

Johnny dove through the window headfirst, twisting his body and whipping out his bow as the two fell from the building.

As they fell, Johnny fired a clothesline arrow, Barney's latest gift, above into an intact portion of the building. The rope tensed.

With the boy firmly held, Johnny shouldered his bow and braced for the recoil. The explosion from the ball dislodged his arrow before that happened, and he fell the last story onto his back.

He grunted. That didn't go exactly as planned. Still, he was alive. He turned to the boy. "You okay, buddy?"

The little boy, trembling, nodded his head. From the corner of Johnny's eye, he noticed cops hiding behind their cars. He made his way over and led the child to the policemen, who'd only just realized the Crimson Arrow was now standing before them.

"Take care of the boy!" Johnny shouted.

"Wait Mr. Arrow!" the child yelled.

Johnny looked back at the boy.

"That was really cool. I'm Sage, by the way." Sage was beaming.

"I'm glad one of us thought so. Stay safe, Sage!"

Immediately, Johnny darted back into the fray, ascended the nearest building, and entered through a window. On the floor of the room in which he arrived lay an older woman, unconscious, presumably from the smoke. Two quick steps took him to her side. Lifting her to his shoulder, he made another trip down to the bewildered cops below. This time one shouted, "Hold!" and watched as the Crimson Arrow deposited the woman in front of them.

Believing he'd gotten everyone out, Johnny remembered Barney's words about not letting what happened to April happen again. When a problem knocked on Mazono's city gates, Johnny had made a vow and had no choice but to uphold it. Thanks to that last heart-to-heart, Johnny was glad to be out here saving the city, and hopefully making April proud.

"Ian," Joey called, "Come over here! Now!"

Excitement fluttered and trembled in the reporter's voice like a bird before take-off. This excitement spread to Ian, who came running.

"Look here, bro! Look! Five hundred thousand views and counting! Look at that!"

"Dude! I can't believe this!" Ian said.

Ian's eyes were on the screen, on their YouView page where they had uploaded the video of the destruction shaking the city of Mazono. At first, his eyes shone with excitement, glimmering brighter than the laptop screen, before the light in his eyes suddenly dimmed as an internal shadow crossed his eyes. It wasn't proper to rejoice at the misfortune of others, even though it would turn out to be good fortune for himself and Joey.

"But..." Ian said, "We should be viewing this news solemnly, even grimly. We shouldn't be jumping up and down as if this horrible tragedy is good news!"

Joey looked at Ian slowly, as if he was seeing him for the first time. Mazono was his home, and the current crisis was one that called for soberness, to think and reflect, and maybe offer a solution. Solution? Who was he kidding? The only reason either Joey or Ian were going near the bombings was in search of fame. Okay, he would give Ian and this disaster a minute of silence. That was all he wanted, was it not? Joey was no superhero. The Crimson Arrow should take this one on all by himself.

What Joey was going to do for the citizens of Mazono was to show them the extent of the trouble they were in. If that caused problems, it would be no fault of Joey's, but rather of the panic-stricken and unthinking citizens. Joey maintained a sad, confused look on his face for Ian's benefit.

"I don't know if we should keep going with this. We look like some heartless opportunists," Ian muttered.

"We owe the citizens," Joey preached. "They have to know what's happening in their city."

"They need to see this horror? What do we have to gain from showing this tragedy, beyond our own fame?"

"We will gain peace of mind. We'll be helping people. People who see this will avoid these dangerous areas because we let them know about the situation. We'll likely save a life that way." Joey's eyes widened so much that they were practically the only things visible on his face. "No! Lives! We're saving many lives, Ian. So, when you ask me what we get from this, know that we get happiness, peace of mind, and the satisfaction that we have saved lives."

"You really think that?" Ian asked.

"No. Not think. I know that. I. Know. This. If we're seen as opportunists, then it's our cross. It's the cross we have to bear."

Ian looked thoughtful, and the furrows slowly disappeared from his forehead. "I guess you're right. It is," he finally said.

If this was how he had to rationalize his mistake with Zbysko and the current situation…so be it. Joey's eyes strayed to the monitor, and he struggled to contain his heart's quest to be freed from his chest. One million views!

Detective Roenega floored the gas pedal of his police-issued Genesis vehicle, his eyes fixed on the road, as a myriad of thoughts ran amok in his head. Sirens atop a horde of police cars blared into the night behind his vehicle. Fire Service vans edged behind those.

Roenega slid out of his car and stared transfixed at the images unfolding before him. It was much worse than what he watched in the amateur Maz-TV video feed earlier. He could barely make out the faint outlines of Big Foods — an eatery he and some of his PD buddies flocked to during break time. As he looked toward the smoky void that snaked to the heavens, he worried for the owner, Mr. Reus.

Suddenly, a fiery ball of orange erupted to the west of where Roenega stood. He flinched, but stopped himself from reacting excessively; his men were standing there with him, depending on him for moral support.

He fished for his coms, held it to his lips, and barked harshly into it. "Spread out. Circle the perimeter, get everyone you can find to safety." He grabbed his .9mm caliber pistol from its holster and cocked it, the reassuring sound calming his nerves.

"Unbelievable," he muttered, watching order crumble before him.

This was bad for everyone. It was bad for the citizens, it was bad for Mazono's image, it was bad for the police department, and it was bad for business. What in the hell was happening? Who was doing this? He and his men stood safely back from the danger zone, wondering what course of action he should take now. Corpses, burnt to a crisp, lay before the buildings where they had fallen. Some bodies were incomplete, with just enough left behind to show they were once human.

"This is ridiculous," Roenega muttered again, wishing he could shoot the bastard that was doing this straight in the face, between his two ugly eyes.

"This is when you need a foolhardy vigilante, who's gonna wade in there, bombs or no bombs," one of the men said.

"Oh yeah? And what? The idiot doing this is just going to sit on a nice old sofa waiting for the Savior to come capture him, eh?" Dusty flared.

"No, but he could save all of those still in the burning buildings. We're accomplishing nothing here," the man replied.

"I see. Maybe you should try on one of those capes and wait for me to gun you down. Lawless vigilante."

The thought of the Crimson Arrow got on Roenega's nerves hard, grating on and on until he could barely breathe in or out. Grating on him until his entire body felt like it was shutting down.

"What do we do, Dusty?" the man asked.

"We do our job," Roenega replied through clenched teeth.

There were no questions, no arguments, nor counter-arguments. Just silence and acceptance. He turned to the wreckage again, and for an instant, he wished he had special powers, wished he was mad like Crimson Arrow and could go anywhere. He pushed that thought from his mind.

Squaring his shoulders, Roenega breathed deeply. As the warm air flowed into his nostrils, he ran into the void.

The Crimson Arrow crept through the shadows, watching for signs of Alana, trying not to think about his pain. Alana had struck him where the Slayer had injured him before. How many more of these mercenaries could there be? The last explosion signalled that Sheath was close.

Johnny knew that Sheath had no problem inventing new ways of lining up corpses to lure out the Crimson Arrow. Johnny had to end that maniac once and for all. Sheath's detonator was reducing the city to debris and sand. Johnny needed to get his hands on it.

Hearing footsteps, Johnny melded into the darkness. A figure approached. As Johnny crept along to get a better view, the figure moved swiftly, the soles of their feet barely making contact with the ground as they slid effortlessly along the dark sidewalk toward a building. Sheath? Had to be.

Johnny followed the shadowy target until he finally had a clear view. *Fuck. That's not Sheath. That's the guy from the hospital.*

Johnny had to find out where he was going. Had to keep an eye on him. The brute strength of the man made him a threat like no other Johnny had yet encountered. If he could shoot an arrow into his brain and end him, he would. There'd be no holding back now. Johnny raised his bow and aimed.

Suddenly, Johnny realized that if he missed, he'd be at the man's mercy. Johnny realized that his own strength and fighting skills were no match for Scooter's. Half a second's hesitation, and the clear shot Johnny'd had was gone. Kicking himself, Johnny watched as the man walked into a building.

Suddenly, a nearby building exploded. Sheath again. That madman would never stop, would he? It didn't take long to notice that the exploded building had taken its toll on the others surrounding it. Fire was creeping over to the building his foe had entered. This gave Johnny an idea.

This better work.

Johnny attached a stun grenade to an arrow and fired it through the door he had seen Scooter walk through. A bright display of light appeared, followed shortly by a bellowing blast of pain-inducing sound.

The impact of the explosion combined with the spreading fires did the trick, and the building ruptured, crashing in on itself. One problem dealt with.

Then the debris started moving.

No fucking way.

This monster was still alive. A bloodied arm punched an opening through fallen sheetrock as Johnny watched, dumbfounded at what he was seeing.

Plan A didn't work, but he still had the advantage. He planted his feet and took a deep breath to regain some composure.

Scooter had reached to grab something stable, but his hand slipped. As he reached for it again, Johnny fired an arrow directly through Scooter's hand. Johnny could hear the howl from underneath the rubble. The hand quickly returned to its host beneath the surface.

Johnny bolted towards the rubble and dropped another stun grenade inside the opening Scooter had created, followed immediately by a smoke grenade.

They both exploded instantaneously. A blinding flash of light and a mountain of smoke emerged from the hole.

The area was now almost completely engulfed in flames. That had to be enough to take him out.

On to his next target! Johnny needed to resume his quest to find Sheath. He turned on the coms.

"Any idea where Sheath is?" he said.

"It's tough to say for sure. Cameras in the area are getting destroyed left and right. That said, there was some footage of him a few blocks west of where you are right now. That's the best I can do right now," Barney replied.

"Thanks," and with that Johnny made his way west.

As he crept past building after building, and looked through them window by window, he found the assassin. Sheath was inside what appeared to be an office, sitting in front of a monitor.

Unfortunately, from this angle, there was no way the Crimson Arrow could shoot him. He'd have to get inside the room. Slowly, Johnny crept round the window and began opening a door, in a way he'd thought would be soundless. Immediately, he could hear Sheath begin to laugh.

Now that Sheath knew someone was in the room with him, Johnny was trapped. His only option was to distract Sheath and make a break for it. Fighting was not an option in here. But how was he to distract someone who would set off explosives if he so much as considered moving? And that gave him an idea. But if that idea was going to work, he was going to have to go for it. Ah, well. So be it.

He went to raise his quiver and immediately felt the force of a tremendous blast knock him savagely to the ground.

"Crimson, brother, ya really don't stop, do ya?" Sheath said, laughing. "Do ya have a death wish? If ya do, I don't mind. That makes my job awfully easy, but it sure took ya long enough to find me. I mean, how on earth do ya…wait, what're ya doing?"

Johnny had managed to pull out his last smoke grenade from one of the compartments in his suits. He threw it directly at Sheath.

"You fooking coward!" he shouted. "You'll never escape me ya bastard!"

While his attacker was still occupied dealing with the effects of the gas, Johnny got to his feet and scurried out through the hole in the wall, doing his very best to keep moving forward. His stab wound had re-opened. Every step, every breath, was agony. The road in front of him was fading in and out of focus, and he stumbled a few times from waves of dizziness.

Stay conscious, Johnny. If you want to stay alive, stay conscious.

Johnny retreated to the nearest alley when he heard what sounded like crying. His mind had to be playing tricks on him, as he faded off and on the brink of unconsciousness.

He tried to ignore the sound, but it came again, this time clearer. It sounded like a woman crying. He tensed. Had she been nearby when the last explosion hit? Was she trapped? He cautiously crept towards the direction where the sound came from, and as he did, he gradually discerned the figure of a woman trapped under some debris, her body pinned down and her face buried in her arms, crying as if her heart would break.

He approached her gingerly, conscious of the fact that he had barely escaped with his life from Sheath. He had no interest in being killed by one of the other monsters out here tonight.

He looked around for any assailants hidden in the shadows, but there was nothing except smouldering buildings and rubble. Well, he couldn't leave a woman trapped like this, especially when there was a madman running around with remote-controlled explosives, could he? The thought of another human life in danger gave him some much needed adrenaline.

"Hello?" he called. The woman continued crying. As he approached her, the light of the damaged streetlight fell on lush, dark hair falling around her face, completely blocking it from view. "Ma'am, are you okay?"

She mumbled, the words muffled by her hands and hair. "Ma'am," he said again, acutely aware of the fact that he was running out of time. "We need to get out of here. It's not safe here. I'm going to help you out." The woman mumbled again, but he couldn't make out what she was saying. Exasperated now, he stepped closer to her.

"Ma'am, please stay still. Our lives are in danger. We need to get out of here." The effects of the tear gas would have worn off, and Sheath was no doubt barrelling down the road in search of him. The woman remained stubbornly huddled, refusing to look up at him. Her crying had grown more intense.

"Ma'am," Johnny said, worried that Sheath would find them soon, but unwilling to leave this woman at his mercy. Finally, even though his instincts told him otherwise, he bent and lifted the debris off of her. "Hey…" Whatever he was about to say fled from his brain as she raised her head and he finally saw her face. Alana!

"I guessed that the damsel in distress theatrics would get you," she said, her voice cold and ruthless. "Men. You're so predictable." With that, she sprang to her feet and lunged into him again with a knife. He barely evaded it, his thoughts racing.

Suddenly, the heady feel of anger cleared his mind. This woman had used a child as bait. Now she thought she could get rid of him, did she? He had other plans.

"Listen," she said, "there's no point trying to get away. I have a lifestyle to maintain, and you're this quarter's funds. I promise I'll make it quick."

"Oh, well isn't that reassuring," said a sarcastic voice from a few feet away. Johnny felt his heart sink. Sheath had found him.

The woman sighed in exasperation as she, too, recognized the voice.

"Victor Sheath," she said, not taking her eyes off Johnny. "What filthy hole did you slither out of? If you get in my way, this will be the last thing you ever do."

"I'm utterly terrified," Sheath replied mockingly. "Now sit on the sidelines like the pre'y girl that ya are and let me take care of this."

"Not today," Alana hissed. "This one's all mine. So get lost."

"Like hell I will," Sheath replied. "I found him first."

"And you let him get away, like the inept slug that you are," Alana retorted. "So he's mine now. Deal with it."

Johnny was between them this entire time, feeling like a mouse caught in between two cats. He decided to do something about the situation while they were still distracted.

In a move neither assassin expected, Johnny rushed towards them. He brought Alana down with a single leg takedown and quickly picked up the knife she dropped.

Recovering seamlessly, in a single motion she slid out another knife and slashed his right side. It didn't pierce him particularly deep, but pain exploded in his side anyway, and he winced.

"Could've told ya he was a sneaky one," Sheath laughed.

"Fuck off," Alana replied.

Johnny heard the sound of running, and rolled to the side in time to avoid a strike from Sheath. As he sprung to his feet, he blocked a punch from Alana, then thrust a knee in her stomach, bending her over and leaving her gasping for air. He heard Sheath charging at him from behind, turned quickly, and met him with a fist to the face. As he did so, he heard bones crunch.

"Dammit!" Sheath shouted. "Ya broke my fooking nose!"

Before Johnny could react, Alana leaped on his back and gripped his neck tightly, her chokehold cutting off his circulation.

Unable to dislodge her or loosen her hold, Johnny threw himself back into the nearest wall, slamming her against it. She grunted in pain, her hold loosening, and Johnny shook her off, then promptly spun round to kick her in the back of the head. Her knees buckled beneath her, and she stumbled to the floor.

"Enough."

Before Johnny could catch his breath, an explosion erupted near him and took him off his feet.

Alana, on the other hand, was back on her feet and rushed at Johnny, attacking furiously, knowing that he was weakened and vulnerable.

"Aren't ya listenin'? I said enough."

Another explosion went off, and the full force blasted into both Johnny and Alana. The two lay together in a bloody heap.

This worked to Johnny's advantage. Alana's body gave him a little cover from Sheath. He was able to grab his bow. He aggressively forced Alana near Sheath, prompting him to detonate more explosives.

The impact caused him to wince, but the distraction was worth it. Johnny fired an arrow through Sheath's hand, causing him to drop the remote. He scrambled to pick it up, but Johnny fired again.

Sheath came charging at him. Johnny braced himself, then used the other man's momentum to pick him up and throw him headfirst into the wall, where he connected and slumped over.

Alana stirred. Although she herself was badly beaten, she still held the advantage over the bleeding Johnny. She rushed him.

As Johnny countered her blows, he thought desperately of some way to quickly overcome her.

He blocked her next strike, grabbed her hand, and contorted her arm as hard as he could, nearly pulling it out of its socket. Then he quickly feigned the snapping of her arm, as he drove her headfirst into the nearest wall.

Undaunted, she recovered swiftly, and turned back to face him. As she madly rushed at him, he neatly sidestepped her assault, dislodged his quiver from his back, and hit her with a precise blow to the back of her head. She fell to the ground, unmoving.

Once she was dispatched, Johnny returned to the inert form of Sheath, searched through his clothing for any other weapons, and then made his way over to what he really wanted: the detonator. He slipped it into his uniform.

"Where the fook do you think yer going?" Sheath was lumbering to his feet. "I'm not done with ya yet Crimson, my boy."

Another rustling sound came from behind him. Alana was stirring as well. This fight wasn't over. Johnny checked his quiver. He had come with twelve arrows, and had fired five thus far. He also had the detonator.

His two foes worked towards positioning themselves on each side of Johnny. He could feel the sweat fall from his brow. He took in a deep breath and prepared himself.

"Well, look who it is. Yer lookin' a lil' burnt there Scootsy. Spend a lil' too much time in the sun?" Sheath laughed.

You have got to be kidding me.

Johnny's heart sunk. He turned around. A black, charred, and disfigured body was slowly making its way nearer. Flesh on the arm of this man had been completely burned through to the point where bone was visible. Yet, he persisted toward the Crimson Arrow and the two fellow assassins.

Johnny had no choice. He couldn't fight them all head-on. He needed to keep them at a distance. He pulled out his bow and fired two shots at Sheath, one piercing his shoulder. Sheath howled in pain.

As soon as the shot had been fired, Alana and Scooter rushed in. Johnny was able to turn around and aim the detonator at Alana and send an explosion her way, taking her off her feet momentarily.

That only left Scooter, who had closed the gap and grabbed hold of Johnny. Just as before, the grip was held with seemingly unlimited strength.

Trying to struggle free proved futile. Scooter's hands moved to the neck of his prey and started choking the consciousness out of him.

Gasping for air, Johnny was running out of time. The coloration of his face was changing, and his vision was getting hazy. The detonator and bow had been knocked loose from his hands.

He scratched and clawed at the charred skin of his assailant, trying to break free. A whip wrapped itself around Scooter's neck, and the grip began to loosen.

"He's mine!" Alana screamed.

Quickly, Johnny grabbed an arrow from his quiver and forced it through Scooter's right eye. His hold released, and his body collapsed.

Alana rushed in, but was blown back by another explosion. Shit, he had been able to pick up the detonator again. Sheath had managed to successfully remove the arrow from his shoulder.

The longer this dragged out, the worse Johnny's chances of surviving were. He needed to escape or end this as soon as possible. He bolted to the nearest building, as Alana and Sheath gave chase.

He dodged chairs, tables, and other furniture as he rushed through the building. Jumping through the window on the other side in a rain of glass, Johnny took three strides before diving behind some rubble, as his fingers reached into his costume and pressed the detonator's button.

Inside the building he had just run out of, explosions popped up one after another with a bright flash and a deafening boom. The building gave way. His foes trapped inside.

Johnny placed his hands on his knees, breathing hard. Now that the immediate danger to him was over, at least for now, the pain was washing over him in waves. He needed to get out of here. He stumbled as far away from the alley and his assailants as he could, hoping they wouldn't come to anytime soon. His body couldn't stand another fight. When he was sure he was as far away as possible, he activated the communications system on his suit. Barney's voice immediately came through, concerned and a little angry.

"Johnny, a lot of the cameras are down. What's your status?"

"Barney…" Johnny said, his vision beginning to blur.

"Johnny?" Barney replied, alarmed. "What's wrong?"

He knew he needed Barney's help to get somewhere safe.

"Direct me…somewhere safe…now. I don't think those guys…are still alive…but I'm not sure."

He struggled to keep his eyes open, to stay alert. He was exhausted.

Keep moving.

"Okay, based on where your signal is…this looks stable…this is where you need to go. It's close."

"I'm going to hang tight there for a bit and recuperate. Then I need you to come pick me up."

"A lot of the routes are blocked off or destroyed. The most efficient way for me to meet you is for you to cross Hollow Alley. It's typically a no-go zone, but with everything going on I can't imagine it will be a problem right now."

"Perfect. I'll see you in a bit."

A few minutes later, Johnny stepped into the building Barney had instructed him to get to. He staggered across the room, looking for a place to rest. Before he could find anything, his legs gave way under him, and he fell down. Every muscle in his body throbbed, and he groaned in pain. Where was he? He didn't even know. He leaned back tentatively and heaved a sigh of relief when his back came in contact with the solid form of a wall. He let his head fall back and allowed his eyes to flutter closed.

I have to stay awake. I have to…I have to stay awake.

His mind began to wander, and thoughts of the good old days flitted unbidden through his head. He was in his apartment, and April was scolding him about drinking too much the night before…now both he and April were drunk and giggling like children while Barney looked on disapprovingly.

"April…" he breathed, as a different kind of pain blossomed in his heart. "How I miss you…"

He felt the wetness on his cheeks, and didn't even try to stop it. Now that his guard was down, the images of that tragic evening came back to him, almost brutal in their intensity. Once again, he was in that garden, so full of hope, anticipation, nerves.

He had spent most of the previous week searching for a ring before he had finally seen one that captured her essence. It was a simple silver band, topped off with an exquisitely cut diamond. There was beauty in its simplicity. It was class, elegance, strength, and vulnerability all wrapped up in one. Like his April.

How many times had he watched her feverishly go through her books during a particularly challenging case? How many times had he seen her go head-to-head with some of the best lawyers in the court room, then go home and simply curl up in his arms, needing his comfort, his strength? How many times had he marvelled at her ability to be strong and assertive, yet fragile and vulnerable?

He sighed. He was what he was now, for her. At first, he told himself that this burning feeling inside him was not rage, but a strong desire to see the city cleaned up as she had wanted. Whenever he caught a criminal and took him to the police station, he told himself that he was doing this for the best of the city, and not because of the guilt he felt about her death. But he did feel guilty.

Since her death, a myriad of questions and 'what-ifs' had tormented him. What if he hadn't asked her and her friends to wait for him at that spot? He had known how volatile the city was; why did he think that place would be any different? Why hadn't he thought of somewhere else? Why hadn't he simply proposed to her over dinner at his apartment or a nice restaurant? Why?

He shook his head to clear the images of April lying in a pool of her own blood, yet looking at him with eyes filled with love. She hadn't blamed him. Till the very end, she just kept on loving him.

But it was all my fault. I should never have left her and her friends alone. I should never have made them wait for me at that damn park.

He was the only one to blame, and the only way he could try to assuage some of his guilt was by ensuring that other people didn't meet the same fate. That was why he was the Crimson Arrow. If he couldn't be there for April, he could be there for other helpless citizens of Mazono. One day, hopefully, he would again come face-to-face with the man who had taken April's life so brutally. Then he would have his revenge.

"I swear it, April," he muttered as his last tenuous hold on consciousness began to loosen. "I'll survive this. Then I'll find him…and he will pay…"

"Johnny."

The voice was soft and alive. He almost felt like he could touch it. There was only one person with that voice. Only one.

"Johnny," she called again.

Johnny turned and saw her staring at him. He tried to make out the expression in her eyes.

"I want you. Come and take me."

She started walking away, her gown dragging after her. He knew she wore nothing beneath. He started after her, watching the gown slip slowly off her.

"Wait," he begged. But she kept moving. He followed her, walking faster, faster, running, running… but he couldn't reach her. She still walked lazily, swinging her hips this way and that. Then she disappeared beyond a cliff.

Atop a roof across the street, a man watched Johnny enter a building through his high-tech mask. He had been on the Crimson Arrow's trail for some time. He'd followed him and witnessed his battle with the madman, the superhuman, and the vixen. He would soon approach his quarry. The Crimson Arrow had proven resourceful and would require further study.

The Omega Archer was a hunter who took great pride in taking down his victims. Though he particularly enjoyed when they were able to give him a challenge. He would allow the Crimson Arrow to live, for the moment, to determine how skilled he might be.

I am intrigued.

When Johnny awoke several minutes later, he stretched, feeling the pain in his bones and muscles. Johnny struggled to get to his feet. It wasn't easy. The evening's battles had taken their toll. He still had multiple open knife wounds. The brief rest he'd managed to squeeze in had strengthened him just the amount he'd needed to get moving.

He made his way across the room and turned on a nearby faucet. He furiously gulped down as much water as he could handle. He was able to find a staple gun and some gauze.

He bit down hard as he stapled his stab wounds shut. The pain was seething. He then redid his bandages. Bleeding out was not how he intended to go, after all he had been through tonight.

Now he needed to get out of this building and head back to the lair, where he could rest and recuperate. Now that Sheath was dispatched, the city was no longer in imminent danger of being blown to smithereens.

Barney had told him he would have to go through the worst part of town and make his way through the no-go zone, specifically, Hollow Alley. So be it.

It didn't take long to reach Hollow Alley. It was just a block or two away from Merrick Street. The area was nearly empty, and only one man remained in the area. The worst of it seemed to be over.

As Johnny made his way past the figure, the man immediately attacked him with a knife. Acting on pure instinct, he jumped out of the way. *Another one? Really?*

His attacker stumbled forward a few steps, regained control of himself, then turned back to face Johnny, still holding on to his knife. In the semi-darkness, lit only by the burning buildings in the distance, the Crimson Arrow sensed the man grinning at him. What? He looked closer, squinting into the shadows, but couldn't see more than vague shapes: a nose, eyes, a mouth. The man charged Johnny again. Narrowly evading the blade of the knife, Johnny grabbed the man's wrist and applied pressure until he dropped his weapon.

In response, another knife appeared from beneath the man's overcoat. Johnny pushed away from the man to avoid the vicious downward thrust of the second knife. As a glint of light off the knife reflected onto the man's face, Johnny finally saw the monster clearly. It was the Slayer. Instantly, Johnny's world turned red. All logic left him.

He needed to kill April's murderer. He sprang on top of the man with no regard to any other weapons he might possess. Growling like an animal,

Johnny forced the Slayer to the ground, kneeled on his chest, and began to punch him, one punch after the other, whipping the man's head from side to side like a rag doll.

"Why did you kill her?!" Johnny screamed.

"I saved her, you fool."

"You murdered the best thing that ever happened to me!"

"I did you a favor, but I can send you over to her right now if you wish," the man teased, following with insane laughter.

"I am going to end you right now. I am going to wipe you off the face of this earth! But first, I'm going to make you suffer!"

"You're such a fool. Like the rest of them. All fools. She was my bride. At the last instant, as she took her last breath, she looked into my eyes and surrendered to me. She said, 'Take me, my love.'"

At hearing these words, Johnny roared. His hands flew to the Slayer's throat, intending to crush his windpipe, when suddenly Johnny felt a knife press into his stomach. He heard a chuckle. "You truly are a fool. You didn't learn anything from our last get-together, did you?

Johnny thought frantically: could he kill the Slayer with one last mighty squeeze before he himself bled out? He put those thoughts to rest. It was clear what he needed to do. He needed to take this man's life. More than anything he wanted…no…he needed his vengeance.

Johnny crawled back, and blood spurt out of his newest wound. His hand reached into his pocket and grabbed the detonator. Arm to the sky, he showed it to the Slayer.

"Do you know what this is? It's the device that's going to kill you. You won't be set free. You'll just disappear into nothing."

He aimed towards the Slayer, and grinned. He put his finger on the button. As he did so, an arrow whizzed directly into the device. He turned to look in the direction it came from. By the time he could look back, another arrow had already flown past him.

The Slayer looked down at the arrow now protruding out of his chest and smiled. *How poetic. I couldn't have asked for a better release. Dear beloveds, I am on my way.*

Johnny couldn't believe this was happening. Where was this coming from? Before discovering an answer, Johnny felt warm blood seep from his hand where the detonator had been.

He gradually came to his senses, and saw the Slayer slumped into a corner, an arrow pierced through his heart. Johnny crawled over to the bedraggled man, swearing as he realized that the eyes he was looking into were vacant and lifeless.

The realization that he had been deprived of his long-awaited revenge tore at him from inside. This was something he could never get back. He could never avenge his failure with April now. That wasn't even the worst part: the bastard was grinning ear to ear. After all the lives he had taken, this monster had left the world happy, and it made Johnny sick to his stomach.

He kicked the empty shell of a body viciously. "Fuck! Why? Why did you take this from me?! Why did you set him free?!" he screamed.

From a building opposite where Johnny stood with the body of the Slayer at his feet, the Omega Archer watched. He had seen the fight between the Crimson Arrow and the Slayer, and he was not impressed.

The man had obviously been in the grip of some strong emotion, and he had allowed that emotion to cloud his reasoning. That, to the Omega Archer, was the highest form of weakness. Therefore, he had taken the kill for himself.

He raised his bow again. This one would be for the kill.

Johnny found himself bombarded by a rain of arrows. With no time to think, he dove behind a garbage can, grabbed the lid, and used it as a shield while his mind raced. He had to get out of here as soon as possible. His attacker occupied a vantage position, and one of those arrows would no doubt do him fatal damage if he didn't escape. He looked around and realized that he was at a dead end. The only way out of here was right through the hail of arrows, and to attempt going that way would be suicide.

Johnny forced himself to calm down and think.

There's a way out, man. Find it!

Johnny wasn't thinking clearly. He'd been easily ambushed by the Slayer and fell into the trap of fighting him, letting his emotions take hold of him again. A fight he could have lost. Until, shamefully, the Slayer was killed for him, not by him. He had to think. He had to free his mind of every other thought, even as he had watched his vengeance taken right out of his hands.

Think, Johnny, think. There's always a way.

Time slowed for a bit, as those words struck a chord and triggered a tingling sensation in his chest.

There's always a way.

It was during one of his father's many MMA fights. His opponent had been a well-muscled man known as the Machine, and he was hammering blows upon blows into his father's frame. A moment later, and the Machine had him in a chokehold.

It seemed the bout would end in the Machine's favor, when Johnny's mother ran up the steps to the side of the cage and yelled, "There's always a way. Everyone has a weakness. There is always an opening."

That had been all his father had needed to hear. Carmichael, Sr., attempted every escape he could until he found one, finally caught the Machine off guard, and was able to transition into an arm bar. When he was able to lock it in, his opponent wailed in agony. It was over in a few seconds, the man tapped out, and his father had claimed victory.

An arrow stuck into the garbage can lid, almost piercing Johnny's forehead, snapping him out of his reverie.

Think, Johnny, think. Find the way.

His eyes roved around the dark.

There!

Just around the bend, a smattering of cars parked in a straight line away from the Omega Archer's vision. *That's it.*

The Omega Archer reached over his shoulder to grab an arrow from his quiver. This was turning out to be a boring kill, and he didn't appreciate it one bit. But money was money, and the bounty on this man's head was substantial. He steadied the arrow on the sling, raised it to his chin, double tapped his foot, and drew it backward.

He released his grip on the arrow, watching it swoosh into the darkness, aimed at the Crimson Arrow's chest. *Interesting.* The boy had thrown the shield — the garbage can lid — at the instant the Archer had fired his arrow.

The lid smashed his bow as his target simultaneously made a break for the cars parked around the bend, away from the Archer's vantage point. The Omega Archer no longer felt in complete control of the situation, and the thought of his kill escaping infuriated him.

I will not allow you to escape, Crimson Arrow. You have not earned that privilege.

Johnny's breaths came in quick, hard successions, as he rested his back on the body of an old abandoned sedan and stole furtive glances around him. He was safe, for now at least. He winced. His body ached, his bones throbbed. How many times had he said that now? Would this night ever end?

An idea struck him, one he had missed the whole *damn* time. He tapped the little dot on the fabric close to his left ear.

"Barney?" he breathed. "You there?"

"Where are you, Johnny? I'm here." The hard voice of his friend filled his ear.

"No time," Johnny snapped frantically.

"What's your status?" Barney barked.

"Hunched behind a car. An archer is somewhere above me. He's dangerous." Johnny could hear the rapid noise of keys being punched into a laptop. He smiled. Barney was trying to locate another way out.

"Okay, I have an idea of where you are. I'm pulling up a map of the terrain." The silence lingered, then his voice came on again. "Okay, there's an old alleyway just a few hundred yards from where you are. If you get there, I'll —"

Johnny severed the connection before Barney finished his speech. He moved slowly. The man had proven himself a fine archer, but could he fight? He hit the button on his bracelet and moved.

Johnny had to be stealthy here. Getting to the alleyway wasn't difficult. But avoiding arrows that could come from anywhere, from an unseen foe, was. He took cover at every opportunity he could before reaching his destination.

The Omega Archer had caught a glimpse of his prey. He had been consumed with trying to locate the vigilante. The area was dense with smoke, and filled with spots that gave adequate cover. Long distance firing was not ideal here. He'd have to make his way down.

He appeared through the smoke, his victim peering directly at him from behind a dumpster. Johnny sprang out, and feigned an anterior strike before attempting to take the Archer's back, where he attempted to fold his arms around the man's neck and apply all the force he could muster.

It was no use. Omega reacted swiftly, lifting Johnny off his feet and throwing him into a wall. *So maybe he can fight.* Johnny rushed at him again, only to meet Omega's knee crashing into his mouth.

Johnny spat. "I didn't know they left the cowards for the end. You afraid to take me on in a fair fight?"

Omega walked closer to Johnny, who struggled to get up the wall behind him. Johnny spit clotting blood onto the ground.

"Nothing to say?" Johnny asked.

"Do you feel owed a response?" said the assassin.

Johnny rushed at him. The Omega Archer sidestepped and shoved Johnny face-first to the concrete.

"You are owed nothing," he said as he kicked Johnny in the face, sending him tumbling.

Johnny stood up slowly and hit out weakly. Omega caught his fist easily and twisted it until there was an audible crack, eliciting groans from Johnny. Another blow sent Johnny crashing to the floor.

As the Crimson Arrow tried to stand, he was met with a boot to the face, sending him fiercely back down to the ground.

Johnny evaded the next blow and managed to get to his feet.

The assassin again went on the offensive, rushing Johnny. They struggled for position and lost balance, tumbling down the alleyway. They continued their back-and-forth until they had exited into a wide open street.

Johnny watched as the Archer's figure stood above him, just staring, the sky behind him an inky canvas. The wind pulsed and lulled, the pattern of it stretching into the dark.

"You took something from me that I can never get back," Johnny said. "You're going to pay for that."

"Unlikely," the figure said, stepping forward.

"Let's go."

In an instant, he was on Johnny, punching. Johnny ducked quickly and retaliated with a punch aimed for the Archer's ribs, but it was easily deflected.

Grabbing Johnny from behind, the Archer flipped him onto the ground. From there, he swirled and kicked Johnny hard in his ribs. Johnny yelped, regaining his feet.

Johnny lashed out, aiming for his enemy's gut, but missed. The Omega Archer swatted Johnny's fist away, landing another punch to his midsection. Driven backward, Johnny found himself at the Archer's mercy. Two more strikes later, Johnny lay sprawling on the ground.

"Let us finish this, Arrow."

Johnny stumbled to his feet, only to be met with an iron fist smashing his jaw, sending him to the ground once again.

Johnny was unable to counter, as the Archer thrust punches into him one after the next, then swirling, smashed his face with a kick. For one long moment, Johnny's body hung in the air, then landed with a thud that shook the ground around him.

Johnny's vision weakened and his bones groaned under his weight. The Omega Archer placed his foot on Johnny's chest. Johnny squinted. It was hard to see, and everything swam in blurs. Each blow had dampened his senses, as raw pain coursed through his veins. He strained to move, but couldn't.

Omega forced his weight onto Johnny's chest, towering above Johnny like a dark hill, his left foot pinning him down.

"You remind me of my youth," the Archer said, pulling Johnny to his feet until their eyes met. "But I don't look back upon those days with pride or joy. No, only disgust." He released his grip on Johnny, grabbed his bow, and reached for an arrow from his quiver.

"With your last breath know this…you are not worthy of the Omega Archer." Johnny blinked at the arrow aimed for his heart, and shut his eyes. Time slowed as he lay numb and immobile, his back pressed to the pavement.

He could see her in his mind's eye, wearing her favorite dress, jumping and swirling around, and urging him with outstretched hands to join her.

This is it.

Johnny's breaths grew shallow. He could hear the smooth sucking sound of the bow being dragged. The pain would only linger for a moment. He welcomed it.

But the sound he heard next wasn't the whizzing sound of the arrow hitting his chest.

It was the sound of his assailant stumbling backwards.

The pain in the Omega Archer's shoulder was sharp and searing. His vision blacked out momentarily as he stumbled back a step, his bow fallen out of his grasp, and the arrow he'd slung flown in the wrong direction. When he looked around, his eyes found Dusty Roenega.

"I appreciate the heads up, vigilante. That bracelet you've got sure is nifty. Backup is right behind me," Roenega said.

The Archer hadn't been paying attention to his surroundings, and that had cost him. An unforgivable mistake. He willed himself forward, the pain impeding his mobility. He blinked, his eyes moving to his left shoulder — the source of the pain — and stared at the bullet hole seeping blood.

Fool. It would not make a difference. The cop's life would end tonight, same as the Crimson Arrow's.

He charged towards Roenega, narrowly evading two more shots and knocking him off his feet, then smashed him downwards on the ground. As Roenega's head bounced off the concrete, his body slumped.

Meanwhile, sirens blaring, two cop cars slid to a stop, as four officers sprang out of their vehicles, their guns drawn.

"Stand down," one said. "Hands up where we can see them."

There was no response. The Omega Archer did not move.

"On your knees! Now!"

"I kneel for no one," Omega responded, blood oozing out of his shoulder.

"We'll see about that. I gotcha," one cop said as he holstered his gun and reached for the Archer's hand to cuff him. In an instant, the cop had an arrow plunged into and out of his throat.

The cop's partner, who stood beside him, couldn't react quickly enough. The Archer swept him to the ground and jabbed that same arrow into his heart.

The other cops fired in retaliation, only to see their fellow officers' bodies used as meat shields.

An arrow grazed the jaw area of his mask. The force did nothing to deter him. *Excellent shot. Near perfect.*

The Omega Archer wiped the blood flowing from his grazed jaw. He looked up to find another arrow peering out of a bow, Johnny's deft fingers drawing the sling.

The Omega Archer paused. His left arm was now useless, but he was being challenged. He would not back down.

The next shot came quickly. Omega leaned into it and took the full force of the arrow directly into his injured left shoulder.

The remaining two cops had foolishly unloaded their weapons, and the Archer went for them as they began to reload. He charged ahead, knowing his foe only had two arrows left. As long as his left side was facing his foe, the damage would be miniscule.

The cop nearest to him reloaded quickest. Reacting in a panic, he wildly missed the two shots he was able to get off. His mistake would not go unpunished, as he was tackled into his partner and lost control of his weapon.

Moments later, the two men were corpses, courtesy of a pair of bullets to each of their brains.

The Archer straightened. He tossed the empty gun to the side. With the cops' blood sprayed across his face, he looked back to the Crimson Arrow.

Johnny looked ahead at this man, no, this machine, who had torn apart five cops with one arm. Doubt and fear were starting to settle in. After everything he had done tonight, all the battles he had fought, all the danger he had been in, it wasn't until this moment that Johnny could feel the familiar sense of freezing up.

When you grew up having everything handed to you, everything came easy, and the things that didn't could usually be bought. It was difficult to tell how competent you were. Was that A in class earned? What about that spot on the football team? Had I really beaten my opponent, or were their other factors behind the scenes influencing these results?

Johnny hadn't taken out these assassins. Sheath's explosions were the main reason that madman, Scooter, and Alana were dead. Without them, he wouldn't have stood a chance. This Archer was the reason the Slayer, the man who handed Johnny his greatest failure, had been killed.

Even when he had faced down three assassins at once, he had been in control of Sheath's detonator, and one of those opponents had one foot through death's door. This Archer was different – he was terrifying. Fear swept through every crevice of Johnny's body, and he began to tremble.

Why am I such a coward?

Visions flashed through his mind. Barney at the lair, telling him he believed in him. April thanking him for saving her from her assailant. Sage and the woman he had rescued this very night. Flash after flash appeared of the men, women, and children he had protected from his missions.

That's right. I made a vow. A vow to protect.

He wasn't only fighting for himself. He was fighting for everyone he loved, lost, sought to protect, and anyone else that inhabited his city. Mazono was his to protect. The losses had piled up over the last year. This fight was to honor them. For Nikki Holden, Lauren Fraser, and Karen Neely. This was for Walt Zbysko, and the cops lying before him. For Fiona and Shelly, and of course, the love of his life, April.

There were still plenty of lives to protect. His parents, Clair and her family, his newest admirer Sage, Detective Roenega, and Barney. The list went on and on. If this assassin was going to take him out, it was going to take everything he had to kill Johnny. There would be no more fear, and no rolling over here. No, he had found his strength in those who believed in him, and in those who had been lost.

The Omega Archer had called Johnny unworthy, and maybe he was at the moment. But if it was the last thing he did, he would fight until there were no questions lingering about his worth for any longer.

It all came down to this. The proud assassin with the useless left arm against the stubborn vigilante with a broken wrist, all sorts of damage that had accumulated across his body, and multiple open wounds on his torso.

Johnny fired his second-to-last arrow at the Omega Archer, who shielded himself again with his left arm.

"Let's do this!" Johnny screamed as he charged his opponent. Omega knew he wouldn't be able to defend with one arm. This would be an all-out offensive.

The two men made contact. They began to trade shots with each other. Blow after blow, each man recoiled and rebounded, not giving an inch.

Back and forth they went, blood squirting from the numerous lacerations amongst their bodies, sweat flowing down through each and every opening, while grunts could be heard with each successive blow.

Their bodies waned, but the strikes continued. Each collision had less force behind its predecessor. Yet, shot after shot, each man came back for more.

Johnny's extra limb advantage was paying dividends. He smashed the Archer's shoulder with a countless number of hooks that were incapable of being defended.

Arrows still protruded from that arm, and a Johnny strike broke one apart. He intentionally grabbed the other one

He forcefully tore it further through Omega's arm and dislodged it. Johnny dug the metal blade deep into his foe's torso, and the assassin staggered back.

"I got you," Johnny said, barely able to get the words out of his mouth. His foe dropped to one knee.

The Omega Archer couldn't process what was happening. How could this man keep going? It was visible to anyone watching that the vigilante was in a tremendous amount of pain. Despite this, he kept coming back for more, despite the various cracks and pops that had been elicited from Omega's various attacks. Now, with one arm useless, and an arrow lodged in his lung, he was fading fast.

Such a disgraceful position to be in. The thought of being on one knee was sickening. There was only one thing left to do.

Omega fought his way back to his feet. He took a step forward, nearly collapsing again, before continuing on.

He braced, and exhaled loudly, as he swung his right arm with all the force he could muster.

Johnny's body couldn't react quickly enough, and in a split second, the Omega Archer's fist connected with Johnny's chin. The impact instantly caused his body to collapse, sending him crashing to the ground as Omega himself stumbled back and tried to remain on his feet.

The distant approaching sirens of the cops caught his attention. Lights pulsed in the distance.

Johnny stammered to grab his bow, wielding it on his third attempt. One arrow left. His vision was fading quickly. The night sky camouflaged the exact whereabouts of the target he knew couldn't be more than five feet away.

He grinned, and managed to force two more words out of his mouth, "I win," before dropping the bow, unfired, and slumping backwards. Everything faded to black.

Johnny had no idea exactly how much time had passed when he came to. Cop cars had flooded the site of his last stand, as his body was being dragged into an alleyway. He looked up to see the face of Detective Roenega.

"Well done," Roenega said, assisting the vigilante to his feet.

"What about the Archer?" Johnny said.

"He got away," replied Roenega.

Barney appeared around the corner of the other side of the alley, wearing a ski mask.

"I can take things from here," he said.

Roenega carried Johnny towards his friend and passed him off gently. "You know, I might have been wrong about you kid. But let's not make this a regular thing, okay?"

Johnny managed a small chuckle and responded, "Sure thing." And with that, he and Barney were off.

The sun burned idly in the crystal sky as a woman in a grey jacket and skirt dashed out of the Mazono Press building. One hand clasped around her purse, her other clutched a parcel to her chest. Her hair moved in the wind as she walked briskly into the parking lot and to her car, a blue sedan parked between two BMWs belonging to her editor-in-chief and HR manager.

Stealing furtive glances around the parking lot, a habit she'd developed on the job over time to make sure no one had tailed her, Ashley Hayes slid into her car and turned the key. The car rumbled and sputtered. Cussing under her breath, she turned the key again. The car grumbled, but this time, started. Quickly switching gears and easing out of the parking lot onto the highway, she drove toward Franklin Street, one of the most densely populated areas of the city. If there was one thing she'd learned, it was that the journalism business was dangerous, and packages delivered in such a manner as this one, with strict instructions to match, posed great concerns for secrecy.

She'd been in her office in the aftermath of the explosions and fires that destroyed so much of the city, satisfied with the first draft of her article on the Crimson Arrow. She was satisfied that she'd managed to throw some choice words into the mix, without being called into her editor-in-chief's office. She knew she represented the small percentage of those who disliked the idea of a superhero — a vigilante — lurking and operating without proper jurisdiction and from the shadows. Getting her article published in the weekend's special bulletin was sure to spur arguments from the different sides of the divide, which might increase the purchase rates for the newspaper. She realized that was good for business, and for her job. She might even finally be able to apply for a raise. *Talk about killing two birds with one stone.*

She'd been about to save her draft on her desktop when James, the company's mailman, rapped on her door and delivered a parcel. It had no mailing address on it, but came with an accompanying note:

Do not bother if seal is broken.

She'd checked to see if the seal was broken. It wasn't. She thanked James, signed his sheet, and dismissed him.

Upon opening the parcel, she'd been surprised to find it contained another wrapped parcel with a note in the same handwriting affixed to it:

Opening this parcel at your office is not safe. For your safety, move to a secure location.

What the hell was this? A prank? She shook her head. Couldn't be. The city was in crisis. It would be unwise and insensitive for anyone to prank her at this time. She read the note again, running her hands over the package, fighting the urge to open it right there in her office. *There are cameras everywhere*, she thought, coupled with the fact that anyone could barge into her cubicle and see what had been meant for her eyes only. Well, it was almost time for a coffee break, offering a perfect opportunity for her to sneak out.

After making four left turns — a trick she'd learned from a YouView channel — and checking the rear-view mirror to see if she was being tailed, she turned the vehicle into a no-parking area. Thankfully, there were no cops in sight to fine her for parking illegally.

Sighing, she grabbed the package beside her and tore off the next seal, spilling the contents of a file onto her lap.

She gasped as her eyes fell on the material: a dozen photographs with accompanying timestamps, some newspaper clippings, and a document. Is this a blackmail stunt? She knew she hadn't done anything worthy of being blackmailed. Yet. But people get blackmailed for little things these days. She looked more closely at the images. A sigh of relief escaped her lips. She quickly glanced around to see if anyone was nearby. There was no one in sight.

Way to go.

Turning to the document, she read the heading.

What do a spa and beauty salon magnate, a CEO of a fleet of retail stores, a judge, a CEO of several restaurants, a gang leader, and a multi-millionaire have in common to induce them to meet together on an off-the-grid cattle ranch?'

She smiled. Whoever the writer was, he was amateurish but good. She quickly skimmed through the contents and surveyed the images carefully, shock registering on her face. Fascinated, she read through the contents carefully.

At 9:54 am, a ranch outside the city was host to several guests among the high and mighty of Mazono.

Eric Marcoso

Philip Johnson

Dean Fletcher

Donna Henshaw

Eric Taylor

Douglas Thompson

She checked the photographs and confirmed the reporter's notations. Different photographs, presumably taken from a remote location, displayed the five persons getting out of their cars at different times, heads bowed low, and walking into the house.

She read the next line.

Six walk in, five walk out. One reported missing the next week.

Ashley counted the images of the dignitaries leaving the compound. There were only five of them, she noticed. *Gavin had said his boss was killed.* She looked for the missing person and found out it was Phillip Johnson. A sickening thought flashed through her mind.

Is this person positing that Mr. Johnson was killed on this ranch?

She read the next line.

Shortly after this meeting was held, a bounty running into millions of dollars was allegedly placed on the Crimson Arrow's head. Coincidence? I think not.

Ashley recounted her talk with Gavin, about the current happenings in the underworld. She remembered how scared he was to reveal anything. She could hear his words pounding in her head, the fear punctuated in every syllable.

"They want him dead. The big guys. They want him dead."

It clicked, as though a lock had met the right key. *So, these are the big guys Gavin was talking about. They were the ones who placed the bounty and killed his boss.*

She checked around the package to see if there was a mailing address she could correspond to, the frustration on her face palpable when she discovered there was none.

Ashley gathered the material from her lap, placed it inside the folder, and dropped the folder onto the passenger seat. She took no notice of the sweat running down her forehead, or at least, paid no attention to it.

This is huge!

Ashley had no idea how to handle this sort of news. She contemplated her options: if she published the materials found in the parcel, the other top guns would refute it, claiming it was doctored or photoshopped, the handiwork of detractors seeking to dent the image of the incumbent government and the name of an influential judge. Her company could face harsh scrutiny. Dirt would be dug up on them. They could be indicted, and she could get fired, or worse, turn up dead somewhere no one would bother looking for her.

In the business of journalism and reporting, she knew that there was no one to be trusted with such information. She knew that in order to tag these high and mighty individuals, she would need more evidence than a couple of photographs and a theory that wouldn't hold water in a court of law.

Ashley slid the folder into the pigeonhole of the car, slid it shut, and fired up the vehicle.

When she arrived back in her cubicle after break, she had a new resolve. She switched on her desktop, and as she waited for the screen to start up, she wrapped her fingers on her glass table, many thoughts filling her head.

She opened her word document software and quickly erased the draft document she'd written on the Crimson Arrow. *I have bigger fish to catch.*

She clicked on the newspaper's database that contained every news article ever published, then typed 'Eric Marcoso' into the search box. Immediately, a 'Loading' sign appeared on the screen. Soon after, search results appeared: a recent picture of Marcoso in a tux, at a ball, took shape at the top left of the page.

She began to take notes.

WHO ARE YOU?

The Lawson University main campus took on a rich tone as the sun hovered over it. A couple of drunken sophomores staggered into their hostels just as the University's security parole drove past. A few students milled about lazily on the lush grounds.

Joey Baker — head of operations, Maz-TV, a YouView channel dedicated to revealing everything from the extreme to the mundane activities in Mazono — sat in the only chair in a cubicle located in a massive edifice that housed students. He drank coffee as his partner and friend, Ian, typed animatedly into a laptop on the top bunk of their bed.

"Dude," Ian said, looking at Joey. "Jamie's throwing a party tomorrow night, and he's invited us."

Joey chuckled, putting his cup on the desk. "We're at the top of the food chain now, my man."

"Should I decline the request?"

"Yeah. Let him beg a little."

Ever since they'd released those bleary images and footage of the explosions on their YouView channel, they had become a worldwide sensation, especially on campus. Subscriptions to their channel had skyrocketed over the past few weeks, the page now boasting over five million subscribers.

Anything they posted received hundreds of thousands of hits. Women who never looked twice at them now waited patiently outside their classes for the opportunity to take selfies with them when they got out.

Weekend parties without Joey and Ian were no parties at all. The two were a force to be reckoned with. Any video they uploaded, from any event on and off campus, became an instant hit.

"Joey, there's something I have to tell you," Ian said.

"Shoot." Joey looked on, as his friend slid the laptop shut. "You've earned the right to tell me anything you want."

Ian shifted. "Ever since we did that bit on the explosions and on the Crimson Arrow, I've been feeling a sense of responsibility to the city."

"Dude, we're doing what we can from the sidelines, and making money while we're at it. Don't you think that's enough?"

"I dunno, Joey, I believe we can do more."

"Like what, Ian?"

"Like go into investigative journalism. Word on the streets was that a bounty was placed on the Crimson Arrow," Ian said.

"So, what are you suggesting?"

Ian looked at Joey, his brows drawn. "Let's go to the streets, speak to some people. Surely, one of them will talk."

"As much as I buy into this *investigative journalism* thing, I frankly think that's a bad idea."

"Bu—"

"No buts, man. The streets are overrun with criminals and thugs, especially here. Talking to the wrong person could lead to consequences. Things that you can't even imagine. Plus, they know us now. We're all over YouView! They'll trace us back to this room, and what do you think will happen then? You think they'll want to listen to your *investigative journalism* rants? Or want to take selfies?"

"Hmm," Ian muttered. "I never looked at it from that angle."

"I know. That's why you have me to talk sense into you."

Chuckles.

"I believe I've talked more sense into you than you've ever done for me, but who's counting?" Ian joked.

"Where are we getting on finding out the true identity of the Crimson Arrow?" Joey asked, changing the subject.

"No meaningful info yet."

Just then, both their phones beeped. They stole curious glances at each other, then both fished for their phones.

"Ho...ly...shit." Joey's mouth flew open.

"This is huge! Fucking huge!"

"Grab your camera, Ian. We want the world to know what's happening, and to get the students' reactions before we hit the streets."

"Wait. Who are you?" Ian said.

Neither of them had noticed the decrepit old man enter their room. They stood puzzled, as he adjusted his bowtie and cleared his throat.

"Good evening, gentlemen. I've been away for quite some time. If you have a moment, I was hoping you two would be kind enough to relay a message for me."

Before they could respond, he pulled a knife out of his sleeve and grinned widely.

The oak trees surrounding the cemetery swayed softly, as though paying obeisance to the dead they hovered over. The sun peeked through the leaves, casting dark shadows on every epitaph. Deep in the woods, the sky blazed blue through the green canopy of the trees sheltering singing birds and humming insects. The temperature had dropped a few degrees, and the air smelled thick with smoke rising from the distance.

"Brethren, we have gathered here to pay our final respects..." A priest in the northeast corner of the cemetery droned in a monotone to a smattering of folks who were gathered around the wooden coffin of a man who had died some weeks after falling into a coma. The coffin was propped onto a platform, a freshly dug grave close by.

The cemetery gardener picked dead roses from the graves, a mournful look on his sallow face. Over at the south corner of the cemetery, two men dressed in matching suits slouched several paces away from a grave.

"You go first," Barney said to Johnny, his voice sounding husky, his face sullen. He stepped backwards just enough to make room for Johnny to talk to April.

Johnny nodded silent thanks and stared wistfully at the calligraphy of the epitaph.

"Hey, April." He could barely hear his voice above the rustling of leaves and the solemn hymn being sung by the funeral mass, but he was sure she could hear him.

"When I started this vigilante duty, this crusade, I had one resolve in mind: vengeance." He paused, took a long whistling breath, and exhaled. "I wanted to avenge your death so badly, I was oblivious to the reality that the city is really falling apart, and it needs a savior. Every step of the way, things became more difficult, and when it became about more than avenging your death — the reason why I started this crusade in the first place — I didn't know if I could keep going."

He blinked back the tears locked in his eyes. "Then I realized that for all your life, however little of it there was, everything you ever did was done to uphold the law and protect the rights of the weak and the defenseless, of the people too afraid to challenge the broken system we have. In your own way, you affected lives, because it was the right thing to do. And that's what I plan to do, April. I want to be the man the city can look up to, and if I can't do it as Johnny Carmichael, I'm sure as hell gonna do it as the Crimson Arrow. My new dream is to honor you by continuing your work. I will fight for what's right and change this city." His eyes fell on the words inscribed on the epitaph:

In Loving Memory

April Smith

Daughter. Sister. Friend.

"I miss you, April."

The winds billowed lightly, as though acknowledging his words. He stepped backward, and tapped Barney on the shoulder. Barney stumbled forward and stood stiffly in front of the gravestone. Barney spoke quietly, inaudibly, to his sister.

Johnny sighed. Barney had been through a lot. He'd always been by Johnny's side, suppressing his pain of losing his only sister, and putting on a strong face in front of Johnny and the press. Now, as he stood at his sister's grave, he looked as battered and dishevelled as Johnny had been when she died.

When he had informed Barney that it was The Omega Archer who put the Slayer down before he himself had the chance to, the look on Barney's face was telling. He was disappointed, but he smiled anyway. It was now a few weeks since the explosions had nearly brought the city to its knees.

Now, as he watched Barney pay his respects to his sister, a daffodil held between his palms, he felt a sense of responsibility to reach out to his friend — just like Barney had been doing for him ever since April's death — and tell him everything will be alright, and that April was in a better place.

After he'd placed the flower on April's grave, Barney moved swiftly toward Johnny, and with deep urgency in his voice, said, "Let's get out of here."

Johnny gave a long hard stare at April's resting place, the daffodil leaning against the epitaph, and sighed. Nodding, he placed his hand on Barney's shoulder as they walked back towards their car parked outside.

"You know," Barney said, breaking the silence and standing facing his partner. "I'm not trying to mince words here, and we've had our fair share of bumps along the way, but Mazono has become better because of the Crimson Arrow."

"This is the part where I'm supposed to blush and mutter thanks, huh?"

"Right."

Chuckles.

"But you seem to be forgetting one integral aspect of this Crimson Arrow crusade."

"And that is?"

"You, Barney. You. I would've been locked behind bars in solitary confinement if not for you."

"I do the little I can, Johnny Boy. I work better behind the desk as opposed to out in the field. I'd look ridiculous in your costume. At least, that's what I picture April telling me."

For the first time in a long time, Johnny smiled. A genuine smile.

And that was when Johnny felt a vibration in his left pocket.

"That's my phone," he said, fishing through in search of it.

"Mine, too," Barney observed, reaching into his own pocket. When he saw the red notification at the top corner of the phone, he stiffened in shock. *What the hell?*

He swiped his fingers to read the notification. Then he looked at Johnny to see that the color had drained from his face as he stared at his own phone.

Johnny barged ahead of Barney, walking hastily to their car parked at the entrance of the cemetery. Barney hurried and caught up with him, gathering his breath.

"Johnn—"

"We've got work to do," Johnny interrupted, throwing the car keys to Barney.

"To the lair?"

"Yes, we need to be prepared for what's coming."

"Agreed, let's go."

The car grumbled and veered off the curb, the sound momentarily interrupting the funeral mass taking place in the cemetery.

Barney swung the car onto the highway and floored the gas pedal. From the corner of his eye, he saw Johnny's jaw tighten.

The text flashed through his head as he swung the car into the parking lot of the gym.

BREAKING NEWS:

Mr. Goode, the man behind the Mazono Massacre, has escaped the Mazono Maximum-Security Prison.

ISBN: 978-1-948842-00-6 (ebook)

ISBN: 978-1-948842-01-3 (paperback)

ISBN: 978-1-948842-02-0 (hardcover)